The Familiar Stranger

THE HEWEY CALLOWAY NOVELS

By Elmer Kelton
The Smiling Country
The Good Old Boys
Six Bits a Day

By Steve Kelton
The Unlikely Lawman

By Steve Kelton and John Bradshaw
The Familiar Stranger

ELMER KELTON'S

The Familiar Stranger

A Hewey Calloway Adventure

STEVE KELTON
JOHN BRADSHAW

FORGE

TOR PUBLISHING GROUP
NEW YORK

This is a work of fiction. All of the characters, organizations, and events portrayed in this novel are either products of the authors' imaginations or are used fictitiously.

ELMER KELTON'S THE FAMILIAR STRANGER

Copyright © 2024 by the Steve Kelton Estate

All rights reserved.

A Forge Book
Published by Tom Doherty Associates / Tor Publishing Group
120 Broadway
New York, NY 10271

www.torpublishinggroup.com

Forge® is a registered trademark of Macmillan Publishing Group, LLC.

The Library of Congress Cataloging-in-Publication Data is available upon request.

ISBN 978-1-250-33113-7 (hardcover)
ISBN 978-1-250-83073-9 (ebook)

Our books may be purchased in bulk for promotional, educational, or business use. Please contact your local bookseller or the Macmillan Corporate and Premium Sales Department at 1-800-221-7945, extension 5442, or by email at MacmillanSpecialMarkets@macmillan.com.

First Edition: 2024

Printed in the United States of America

0 9 8 7 6 5 4 3 2 1

To Boone Bradshaw, my son.

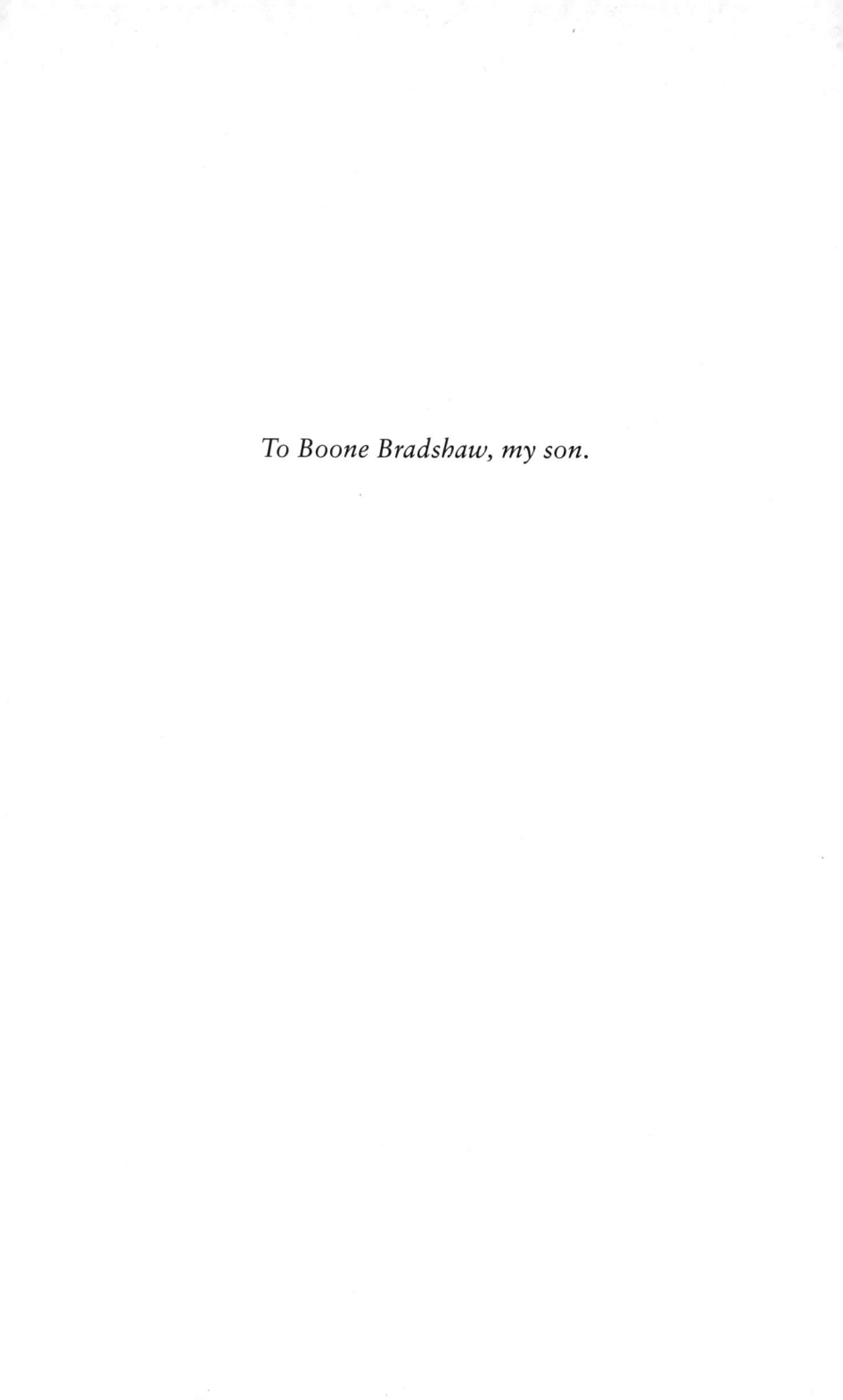

The Familiar Stranger

CHAPTER ONE

Hewey Calloway was looking forward to a café breakfast, even if he had to wait around until after daylight for it. In Hewey's profession such a waste of early morning hours was considered shameful. Townsfolk had more leisurely habits, he reasoned, and it was no more his place to criticize them for their habits than it would be for them to object to his scuffed and worn boots.

He had spent the night at the wagonyard in Durango, intending to pass straight on through town on the way to visit his friend Hanley Baker several miles to the northeast. That plan meant he would be cooking his own breakfast, and he would freely admit to being a lousy cook. A café meal sounded much more to his liking, especially at the little establishment he knew from previous experience turned out an excellent pan of biscuits.

He had eaten little but his own cooking for some time and would be obliged to eat plenty more soon enough, so he sat on the edge of the plank porch outside the café, watching the sun peek over the mountains to the east. His brown horse stood balanced on three legs, saddled and tied to the rail several feet down the porch.

Hewey was a West Texas cowboy who tried not to think too much about his age, but he could not help but notice that he didn't recover as well as he did in his youth.

Anymore a bad wreck or a good night in town was harder to

get over, and since turning thirty several years back there had been a slight stiffness in the morning, and that was on the *good* mornings. Not enough to change his ways, by any means, but certainly enough to notice.

He had left his home range about a year before, bound for Durango with a herd of young horses that his old friend Alvin Lawdermilk had sold to a Colorado ranch. It was supposed to be a relatively straightforward affair; deliver the horses, collect the payment, and return home with the money.

Things got out of hand, however, and here he was in Durango a year later with plans to go north rather than south. Oh, well, he had reasoned, he had always wanted to see new country, and this was a good opportunity to do just that.

The idea of seeing Canada had always appealed to him, although he couldn't have explained exactly why, not even to himself, other than it was a place he had never been.

And that had always been reason enough for him.

※

The street was dimly lit by electric streetlamps that hung suspended by overhead cables. Light glinted off a pair of small railroad irons that ran down the center of the dirt street. Hewey had heard there was an electric streetcar in town, but so far he had not seen it.

Light suddenly spilled onto the porch from behind him, and Hewey looked around to see that a middle-aged couple, probably man and wife, had entered the café from the back and were hustling around preparing for the morning rush.

Soon the lady noticed him and unlocked the door, beckoning as she did for him to come inside.

Hewey had just finished ordering when he caught sight of a familiar face and form; La Plata County Chief Deputy Frank Wiggins was making his way to Hewey's table. Wiggins had reddish-blond hair and a mustache to match it. Hewey had spent a good bit of time with Wiggins the previous year during the trouble with Billy Joe Bradley. The two men had become friends of a sort.

"Is there room for two, Mr. Calloway?"

"You bet, and the name's just Hewey. I have to warn you, though, there won't be a biscuit left in the house by the time I've had my fill."

"Looks like we're leading up to a rassling match, then," Wiggins said with a broad grin, "because I'm partial to the biscuits here myself."

The waitress, unbidden, brought Wiggins a cup of black coffee and asked if he would like his usual breakfast, which he did. There were not that many choices anyway.

Wiggins sat in silence for a moment, a serious look on his face. "What I have to tell you may spoil your appetite, but you deserve to know. Billy Joe Bradley won't be causing any more trouble on this earth."

"Nothing wrong with that news," Hewey replied seriously, his mouth partway full of sausage.

"It's the second part you won't like," Wiggins said. "He found a way to cheat the hangman."

Hewey's face turned grim. "What happened?"

"When it was time to transfer him, the penitentiary sent two guards. The guards and Bradley rode in the caboose so there wouldn't be any danger to innocent passengers if something went wrong. And it did.

"Bradley somehow disarmed one of the guards. It was a suicide move with the other guard sitting right there and still armed. Bradley made a move toward the second guard with the pistol, who had no choice but to shoot him. The guards said Bradley died with a smile on his face."

Hewey sat staring glumly at the table for a full minute or more; then his usual grin reappeared. "I don't like the news," he said, "but I'm glad you told me. That son of a bitch is dead, and I guess that's all that matters. And I'm especially glad you told me here, where I can bury my grief under a pile of good biscuits. Hanley Baker will have to hear about it over my cookin'—or worse, his own."

The two men stood on the plank porch outside for a few

minutes after breakfast, each enjoying a hand-rolled cigarette, and then Wiggins offered his hand. "It's been a pleasure, Hewey," he said. "But next time you come through here, leave the excitement elsewhere, would you?"

Hewey took the deputy's hand and grinned. "Don't you worry. I stay so far out of trouble it never even knows I'm around. This whole deal here was a pure rarity for me."

"Sometimes I believe you might tell a windy now and then, Hewey. I'm thinking this might be one of those times."

CHAPTER TWO

Hewey left Durango at a trot, headed basically northeast along what was more a trail than a road, although it was just wide enough for the occasional wagon that passed through headed to the homesteads and ranches scattered throughout the mountains. The real traffic, if any could be termed traffic, stuck to the main road a few miles farther east that led to settlements higher in the mountains. The trail Hewey traveled wound through a wide valley surrounded by soaring mountains on either side.

Hewey could identify nearly every type of tree, grass, or cactus in West Texas, but he hadn't yet learned exactly what these Colorado trees were called. He knew they were pine, and he knew they were taller than any tree he had seen since leaving East Texas with his younger brother, Walter, two decades earlier.

"Biscuit, it's time for us to find some country where we can see a little ways," he said. Like many cowboys, Hewey would occasionally hold a conversation with his horse. He was a talker, and there were times when his horse was the only one around to listen. "Sometimes I get to feeling a little closed in by these mountains and trees. Kind of gives me a funny feeling."

The storm had come up quickly, as they are prone to do in mountain country. Rain began to fall, thunder was rolling, and Hewey could see bright flashes of lightning against the darkening sky.

He remembered a cluster of cows he had come onto once.

They were burned to a crisp because they made the mistake of brushing up under a tree in a storm. He'd heard that lightning almost always struck the tallest tree in the vicinity, but these trees all towered over him, and he had no idea which one was the tallest. His skin prickled at the thought of such a blazing demise, and the more his skin prickled, the more he thought about it.

Soon he caught the smell of smoke on the wind, which was blowing straight into his face. Either the forest was on fire ahead of him, in which case he desperately needed to be somewhere else, or there was a house up ahead. He thought the smoke smelled like dry wood. It was coming from a fireplace or a stove. He hoped.

Hewey came up on a cabin in a small clearing made up of only a couple acres. A crude barn and lean-to stall with a log-rail pen stood near the cabin. He was still some miles shy of where he expected to find Hanley Baker, but any place would do if it would keep him out of the weather, which was becoming worse.

It seemed that lightning was striking all around him. The old saying about lightning striking the tallest object had made him nervous when he was under the tall trees, but crossing the clearing toward the cabin and barn he was even more nervous. Now *he* was the tallest object. Hewey urged Biscuit into a fast lope to shorten the time they were exposed.

To both his surprise and elation, he and Biscuit made the shelter of the barn without being struck. He unsaddled Biscuit and turned him loose in the lean-to. There was evidence of recent activity in the barn, although not much of it. There were horse tracks but no horse. Hewey studied the cabin as best he could through the rain but saw no movement. He was soaked and cold and wanting a fire, so he sprinted to the cabin door, paused on the small porch, and knocked.

"Go away!" came a hoarse voice from inside. "Ain't no place for anybody here."

"But it's stormin' out here," Hewey answered. "Surely you won't turn a man away in this kind of weather."

"Go to the barn!" The voice was weak but emphatic.

"Just come from there. It leaks somethin' terrible."

"There's things worse than water down your collar."

Thunder cracked near enough it made Hewey jump, and the image of those lightning-struck cows popped into his head. Tired of waiting for an invitation, Hewey forced the door. The smell hit him immediately, but he was already inside. The cabin was small and had only one room, which contained a small kitchen, an ancient wooden table with two chairs, and a sagging bed.

The only occupant was a lone young man lying in the sagging bed. The man tried to rise, but he made only an inch or so before wilting back into the bed. All Hewey could see was the man's face, which was gaunt and covered in angry bumps that appeared to be filled with fluid. "Get out. I've got smallpox," the man said quietly but firmly.

Hewey felt like he'd been kicked in the belly by a horse. His back was pressed to the door, and he would have backed farther had there been room. He didn't turn and flee, although he sorely wanted to. Hewey had never been close to smallpox, but he had heard some awful stories over the years.

Since Hewey was a small boy there hadn't been much that really scared him, neither man nor beast. But the thought of smallpox frightened him terribly.

"I tried to warn you off, mister, but you wouldn't listen." The man lay wrapped in two blankets but was still shivering violently.

"How long have you been like this?" Hewey asked quietly from across the room.

"Don't know," the man answered weakly. "Sometimes I wake up and there's light through the windows. Sometimes it's dark outside."

"So you've been here for days," Hewey said. "Who's takin' care of you?"

"I'm on my own," was the reply. "Couple of little girls been keepin' the bucket outside full of water from the stream. They run and hide before I can get out the door, but I saw them once through the window. I fetch water from the bucket with a lard can when I'm able."

"What about food?"

"Don't recall the last time I ate. It's been a while. I had some old biscuits and a little jerky, but it's gone. I haven't been able to fix anything else. Now, like I told you before, you need to go. You don't want this."

"If I was to leave, you'd die right there in that bed," Hewey told him bluntly, "and I don't want you on my conscience. You've got help now whether you like it or not."

The man just shook his head, too weak to protest further. Hewey, for perhaps the first time in his life, wondered briefly if he was being foolish.

The sick man closed his eyes and fell into a fitful sleep. He wasn't the first person to tire after an argument with Hewey Calloway, nor was he likely to be the last. The rain continued outside, although the thunder and lightning grew distant as darkness fell. Standing on the porch, Hewey ate a couple stale biscuits out of his saddlebags. He had a few supplies of his own, but a quick inspection of the cabin showed meager supplies at best. Hewey knew he would need to look for something more substantial in the morning.

The porch was damp, but Hewey unrolled his blankets there rather than inside the cabin. He was close enough to hear the man should he be needed. Hewey had slept as many nights outdoors as in, although mostly by necessity rather than choice. In this case it was choice. A smallpox patient wasn't Hewey's idea of the perfect roommate. The cabin was also in need of some cleaning. The man obviously had not been able to take care of himself in his weakened state, and Hewey would have to tend to it in the morning, like it or not.

Hewey was up before the sun the next morning. He tended to Biscuit first, feeding him some oats he found in the old barn.

Later he'd stake the brown horse on some green grass. "Biscuit, I don't know that I've ever wanted to saddle up and move on more than I do right now. But I reckon we better stick for now."

The sick man was sleeping, and sleeping well considering the circumstances, Hewey thought. He left the door open to let in some fresh air, and he cleaned as best he could with so few resources. Cleaning suited Hewey less than farming, but he saw no alternative. He felt better knowing no one saw him do it. He checked his patient again. The young man didn't seem to have a fever at the moment, so Hewey took his carbine and slipped into the woods in search of something they might could eat.

※

The deer Hewey shot was a young doe. He never had been much of a shot with a pistol, but he was a fair hand with his carbine, good enough at least to keep himself fed. He wrapped most of the carcass in the tarp from his bedroll and hung it in the barn for protection against scavengers and other varmints. He hauled a hindquarter into the cabin. The man—Hewey still didn't have a name for him—lay still and quiet as Hewey carved off two slabs of meat and eased them into the hot grease in his frying pan.

As Hewey cooked, he checked on his patient. The man had been fevered earlier, but Hewey's nursing skills, poor as he knew them to be, had worked. Cold compresses torn from an old flour sack had broken the fever, and the man roused from his fitful sleep.

"Is that food I smell?" he asked in a low voice.

"Venison," Hewey replied. "You need to eat a bit, and we'll see how it sits before we try some more."

"God, I sure am hungry."

"Ain't much to work with here, but I found a couple of pans, so we'll have gravy to go with the meat, and biscuits of a sort, too. I ain't the best cook."

"Don't know how much I can handle, but I'm sure gonna make a stab at it."

"By the way, what do I call you? My name's Hewey Calloway."

The man in the bed hesitated for a few seconds before replying. "Wilson. Bob Wilson."

Hewey had known a few men over the years who answered to names their mothers never called them. He was pretty sure he could add Bob Wilson to that list.

※

Hewey had been at the cabin about a week and a half by his reckoning, though it had seemed like a month. He wasn't accustomed to spending so much time indoors or staying in one place so long, and the itch to move on, to be horseback and gone, was becoming hard to resist.

During his stay, the pustules he had first seen on Bob Wilson's face and body had gradually scabbed over. Many of the scabs were now falling off. Wilson's bouts of fever had largely faded as well. The man had been up frequently, and when Hewey returned from a short hunting trip, he found Wilson outside, soaking up the summer sun.

Hewey guessed Wilson's age at somewhere in his early to midtwenties, although Wilson sure had not volunteered that or any other information of much importance. He was a grown man, but just barely. He was handsome in a youthful way, a hair taller than Hewey, and slim. He had the look and clothing of a cowpuncher, but he had passed up several opportunities to talk about it.

"You must be feeling better," Hewey said after hanging the fresh venison in the barn.

"I'm back from the dead," Wilson answered. "I've seen smallpox sweep through the mining camps around here, but I've been lucky enough to avoid it until now. It's bad stuff, killed about a third of those who got it, is what I heard. We spent a lot of time digging graves."

It was the first time Bob Wilson volunteered anything from his past, and he didn't offer anything more. Wilson had been friendly and thankful. Hewey couldn't help but like the man but also couldn't shake the feeling that there was more to Wilson than met the eye.

"If you think you're up to takin' care of yourself now, I have somewhere I need to be," Hewey said.

"I do, too," Wilson replied. "Don't suppose you've seen a gray horse grazing anywhere nearby on your hunting trips?"

"Found him the second day and figured he was yours. Led him back and been feedin' him a bait of oats every evening along with mine."

Even at a distance, Hewey thought he saw a quick flash of concern on Wilson's face when he mentioned the oats.

"There was an old wooden grain bin with some oats in it. They're a little old, but they haven't gotten wet and molded," Hewey quickly added. "The one part of the barn roof that doesn't leak seems to be right over the grain bin.

"Your gray should come drifting in a little before dark of an evening for his daily handout," Hewey continued. "You can pen him whenever you want to."

He had been carrying on the conversation as he walked from the barn. When he got close, Wilson gave him a long, hard look, almost like he had never seen Hewey before.

"You and I both have places we need to be," Wilson said, still studying Hewey closely. "But it doesn't look like either of us is going anywhere for a while. You've got the rash, cowboy. The fever is bound to follow directly. You did me a good turn, and now I owe you. You're about to start collecting."

CHAPTER THREE

As far back as he could remember, Hewey had seldom been sick. His lifestyle kept him away from towns for weeks at a time, which limited his exposure to the ailments that periodically swept through the settlements.

This left him ill-prepared for the fever that seized him, along with the rash. He had never experienced anything like it, not even close. He alternated between spells of bone-numbing cold and forge-like heat. With the high fever came a sort of delirium that spared Hewey from conscious awareness of much of the hot and cold spells. He was fairly certain Wilson was attending to his hot spells with a cold cloth, as Hewey had done for him before.

That impromptu turn as a nurse seemed long ago, and for all Hewey knew, it had been weeks. He had no recollection of eating during the intense part of the fever, and now his empty belly was gnawing on itself.

"Glad to see you coming back around," said a voice he recognized as belonging to Wilson. "Reckon you could eat something? Sorry to say, I'm no better cook than you, but I have a little leftover dinner I can warm up."

It took effort to speak. His throat felt dry and raspy, and he had very little strength. "I could eat it cold and not complain."

"That's a good sign," Wilson replied. "Means you've about

got this thing whipped. In the mining camps, we seldom had to bury the ones that made it this far. Got to where I was cheering those old boys who made it through, because I was damned tired of helping dig graves."

"That was considerate of you," Hewey managed. Wilson smiled, just a little, for the first time.

Once he had eaten a bit, Hewey faded back into a fitful sleep. Each time he woke up his mind was a little clearer. He remembered developing the same angry-looking pustules he'd observed on Wilson, then seeing them turn to scabs just as Wilson's had done. Many of those, in turn, had been flaking off.

Gradually he began getting out of bed, testing his legs until he was able to sit outside and soak up some sun. Wilson came and went on his own schedule, often saddling the gray, riding off and returning with fresh venison.

Neither man had a lot to say to the other. Hewey never shied away from a chance to talk, but he had trouble corralling his thoughts well enough to carry on a conversation.

Wilson was friendly enough but no more voluble, and he tended to keep his side of their limited exchanges brief and often a bit cryptic.

One evening Hewey's horse came in for his handout of oats before Wilson returned. Hewey felt strong enough to walk to the barn, where he found the grain bin far more depleted than he expected. Unless Wilson was seriously overfeeding the two mounts, the oats shouldn't have gone down nearly that far since Hewey last saw them.

"Biscuit," he mused to the brown horse as he poured a can of feed into the wooden trough, "you don't reckon Bob Wilson had something buried in there, do you? When I mentioned the grain bin the other day, he looked a little bit like a dog caught with chicken feathers in his mouth. I thought he was worried that the oats might be spoiled. Now I'm thinkin' he was worried that I might've found something he didn't want found."

When full dark came and Wilson still wasn't back, Hewey

knew he was gone . . . along with whatever he had been hiding. Well, he thought, the two of them were even, so Wilson's secret would remain a secret, at least to Hewey.

He spent another couple of days resting up, then penned Biscuit when he drifted in for feed one evening. He and the brown horse would leave in the morning.

<hr />

At daybreak Hewey was tying up his bedroll, preparing to head out, when he heard a loud voice from outside.

"Hello the house! Whoever's in there, show yourself!" The voice was commanding and not a bit friendly.

Hewey opened the door and stepped out onto the broken-down little porch. He saw better than a half-dozen riders arrayed in front of the cabin, all armed to the teeth. They were not pointing those guns at him, but they were all casually standing ready. That prompted a momentary urge to jump back inside and bar the door, tempered by a sudden recollection that the cabin door didn't even have a bar.

"What can I do for you?" Hewey asked the man who appeared to be in charge.

"The name's Murphy. I'm with the Pinkertons." Hewey took an immediate dislike to the man who called himself Murphy. He dressed more like a town dude than a cowboy or lawman, but it was his manner that rubbed Hewey the wrong way. He had small, mean eyes that made Hewey mistrust the man instantly. Hewey had always felt he could read a horse by its eyes, and in his experience the same usually worked on a man.

"We've been trailing a bank robber for better than two weeks, and we received information that he was holed up near here. Maybe in this very cabin. For all we know, you're him."

"You got the wrong man," Hewey replied, "I'm Hewey Calloway. But I suspect I might've spent some time with the feller you're after." Hewey explained how he came to be there and to become well acquainted with their quarry.

"Smallpox, you say," answered the Pinkerton man.

"Yes, sir," Hewey replied, "and I don't know that it's done with me yet. I may still be catchin', so it looks like we've got us a Mexican standoff of sorts. I ain't the man you want, but you can't take my say-so for it, and you also can't arrest me without riskin' smallpox. Looks like this could take awhile, so if you don't mind, I'm gonna sit down. You boys probably want to step down and loosen your cinches so them horses can blow a little."

The Pinkerton man held a little private parley with the others. One of them loped off on the same trail Hewey had ridden in on.

"It probably won't be as long as you think, mister. There's a fellow who can clear up this whole thing in a hurry, once he finally gets here. The banker got a good look at the man we're chasing, but he isn't much accustomed to riding horseback, so he falls behind a lot. We'd have been here considerable sooner if he hadn't held us up so.

"Once he identifies you, we'll figure out how to take you into custody without getting close to you." Hewey had the feeling the man called Murphy would not have an issue shooting him on the cabin porch to save the hassle of an arrest. He began to bristle, as he often did when he felt he was being prodded unnecessarily. The cold look on Murphy's face forced him to stay seated on the porch, though.

"Your laggard will tell you quick enough that I'm not your man, so there won't be any need to arrest me at a distance, however the hell you might figure to do it. Never knew I could be such a bother to anybody, at least not by accident."

The Pinkerton man only glared, not speaking. The other posse members gathered together, separate from Murphy, and talked quietly among themselves. The Pinkerton man Murphy kept his eyes on Hewey and did not attempt to associate with the others.

"What is the name of your bank robber?" Hewey asked Murphy after a couple minutes of awkward silence.

"That's none of your affair, cowboy." Murphy looked at Hewey with a challenge. "What did the man call himself, the one you say was here with the smallpox?"

"That's none of *your* affair, Pinkerton," Hewey replied. He thought for a moment the detective might shoot him for it, and he figured Murphy sure would have had the other men not been there to witness it. Hewey kept quiet after that, an oddity for him.

It took about an hour, but two figures on horseback finally appeared in the clearing. Only one of them looked comfortable horseback. When they reined their mounts to a stop, the Pinkerton man motioned to one of the men and pointed at Hewey.

"Here's your bandit, Mr. Booker. I just need you to make it official so I can arrest him."

"That man?" asked the disheveled latecomer that Hewey had pegged as the banker. Like Murphy, he looked and sounded like a transplant to the area. He was dressed more for the bank than for the trail, and he appeared to be supremely uncomfortable.

"Yes, sir," said the Pinkerton man, showing deference to the rotund banker. Hewey wondered about that, since Murphy had not shown an ounce of deference to anyone else.

"I've never seen this man before in my life."

The Pinkerton man let out an audible sigh. "Looks like we have some more miles to cover."

"You're getting paid for this," said one of the townsmen, "but most of us have families to get home to. We've been out longer than any of us intended."

"That's a fair point," said the Pinkerton man.

"I'm staying with you, Murphy," Booker said. "It was my bank and my responsibility."

The palaver went on, and the longer it went on, the fewer men remained to participate. Several of the posse men had come along in hopes of recovering their own money that had been in the bank, but now many were realizing that what little savings they had deposited were not worth this seemingly fruitless effort. After a while Booker and the Pinkerton man rode on, alone.

It was the strangest law enforcement scene Hewey had encountered, but then again most of his dealings with the law had more to do with drunk cowboys than bank robbers. Still, he couldn't figure why the banker stayed on the trail when he was so obviously uncomfortable on a manhunt. But then, Hewey thought to himself, he could never understand a man who chose to sit at a desk all day and count money. Money, Hewey had always thought, was meant to be spent rather than saved.

Hewey thought of the good turn the young Bob Wilson had done him, nursing him when he evidently needed to be riding on. He remembered the good gray horse Wilson was riding when he left.

"He was ridin' a sorry-lookin' sorrel with a blaze face and socks on both hinds when he come here and when he left," Hewey yelled helpfully. "Seemed a nice enough ol' boy to me. He could have gone off and left me on my own long before he did. He had to know there would be somebody after him, but he still stayed until I was able to get up and take care of myself. Don't know whether to wish you boys luck or not."

※

Hewey had heard talk of germs. He didn't understand the idea too clearly, but he imagined that they were tiny creatures bent on doing harm to the innocent and the wicked alike. As he drank from a cold mountain stream, he hoped he wasn't sending too many of those things downstream to cause others misery. Maybe the vicious little critters would be too few and too scattered to do much damage, he reasoned.

The trail toward Hanley Baker's place led Hewey past a cabin in a clearing, much like the one he'd spent so much time in. The cabin was small and plain, as was the barn and corrals. There were several acres broken out in cultivation, ready for either a small field or a large garden.

As he approached, a hard-looking man stepped away from a shed. He held a shotgun in the crook of his left arm, and Hewey could see his right hand was tense where he gripped the stock.

"You come from that sick house?" he asked. There wasn't so much as a feigned friendliness in his voice; it carried a stern edge.

Hewey reined Biscuit to a stop, uncertain where the conversation was headed. "Been there."

"Well, don't be slowin' down," the man said. "I got a family, some young'uns, and we don't need no smallpox here. Just keep on goin'."

Hewey caught movement near the cabin; two young girls peered at him around the corner. He recognized them as the pair who had taken turns filling the water bucket at the cabin when Wilson was gone for a while and Hewey was too weak to help himself. The youngest quickly ducked away, and the older one had fear in her eyes.

He wondered if the father knew about their kindness and quickly concluded that he did not. Hewey decided it was best to leave it that way.

"Don't mean to bring any harm to you and yours," he said to the man with the shotgun, then neck-reined Biscuit off the trail a ways, giving the homestead a wide berth. He imagined he could feel the man's eyes on his back as long as he was in view, and the thought of those twin shotgun barrels trained between his shoulder blades raised hairs on his neck.

Late in the afternoon the trail broke from the trees and Hewey saw Hanley Baker's cabin ahead. He had visited Baker briefly the previous fall, so he was familiar with the place. The cabin was small but stout, made of logs laid horizontally with mud for chinking and a shake roof. There was a small shed next to a corral, all made of the same pine. Like so many other places Hewey had been over the years, more labor than money had been spent in the building of it.

Out of good manners, and also a sense of self-preservation, Hewey reined up well away from the cabin. "Hello the house!" Hewey yelled. "Baker, Hanley Baker?"

"That you, Calloway?" said Baker as he stepped out the door and put his hat on. "Come on in."

"Don't reckon I should," Hewey answered. "I've had the smallpox, and I may still be catchin'."

"Not to me," Baker yelled back. "I had it years ago, and you ain't supposed to take it twice."

"You sure?"

"Sure enough to call you in."

At that Hewey eased Biscuit forward. Baker stepped off the porch and met him partway, extending his hand to shake.

"I'd figured on seeing you weeks ago," Baker said. "Now I reckon I can guess why you didn't turn up. I have a shed and pens around back. Come on; I'll show you."

Hewey gave Baker a brief version of his story, but he was still hazy on a lot of the particulars himself. He never mentioned Bob Wilson's name, because he saw no point in identifying him by what was surely an alias.

Baker listened carefully, thinking it all an odd turn of events. Some portions of the story did not make perfect sense to him, but he attributed it to Hewey's smallpox and the confusion he knew went with it. The rest he attributed to Hewey just being Hewey.

"You're just in time to turn right straight around and go back with me if you're of a mind to. After a long winter I'm about out of staples."

"The way you cook I probably won't eat much anyway," Hewey joked to his old friend. Their mutual lack of skill with a pot or pan was a running joke between them.

"You remember last fall when we talked about Canada?" Hewey asked that evening, sitting at Baker's modest kitchen table. They had a small fire in the stove and the cabin door propped open to let in the cool mountain air. It was pleasant. Baker had produced a bottle of whiskey—kept solely for medicinal purposes, he told Hewey—and the two had enjoyed a few drinks after their bland meal.

Baker sighed. "Yes, I remember about Canada. You talked my ear off one night about it, kept me from sleepin'."

"Well, I'm goin'," said Hewey, with the sort of reckless determination that often led to trouble for him and those nearby. "I didn't spend much last winter, livin' in that line camp, so I've got some of my pay left over. I want to see some new country that's not filled up with fences and towns. We could rope us a moose or maybe a polar bear."

"I don't know about no polar bears," Baker replied. "But we can find you a moose a hell of a lot closer than Canada."

They sat in silence for a minute, each thinking about it. "Well?" demanded Hewey.

"Well what?"

"Are you coming? You might as well. You're not far from the rocker. Better have some fun while you still can."

Baker scratched his cheek, still thinking about it, then sighed audibly. Hewey began to grin.

The next morning the two saddled up in the dark and headed back down the same trail Hewey had just traveled. Baker still had his good bay horse, and he took along an ill-mannered little gray pack mule that had kicked Hewey in the leg that morning for no apparent reason other than meanness.

"That mule better mind his manners," Hewey told Baker. "I don't hold with mules kicking me, unprovoked. I might feed him to the bears, he does it again."

"You'll be packin' your own grub if you do," Baker said. "You can't fault Little Jim for being a good judge of character."

Hewey looked back as they rode away from Baker's cabin. "How'd you end up with this place, being from Texas? Meant to ask you that when I was here before but I forgot."

Baker was a retired Texas Ranger, and Hewey knew he had spent his life in Texas.

"This was my uncle's place," Baker replied. "My daddy's only brother. Thomas Baker. He left Texas, oh, maybe thirty years ago for Colorado to strike it rich, which he never did. But he made enough to buy half a section and build his little cabin on it. He was a bachelor with no kids of his own. We didn't even know he'd died 'til one day I got a letter from the courthouse here sayin' he'd left the place to me. That was three years ago."

"He had another nephew, my brother, Jim." Baker smiled at Hewey. "Guess Uncle Thomas didn't like Jim much."

"My family never owned enough to leave to anyone, but if they did they'd probably leave it to someone besides me, too. I'd be like your brother, Jim."

"Well, I spent a lot of time up here over the years," Baker said. "Growing up I'd come spend part of the summer helpin' my uncle, and then I kept on after I was growed up, when I could get loose. That's how come I know so much about the place, and the whole area I guess."

"Hell of a deal," Hewey said. "It's a nice place. You going to stay up here or go back to Texas?"

"Oh, I'll probably go back to Texas sometime soon. I love it up here where it's cooler and rains more'n once a year. But it sure ain't home."

Hewey felt a touch of homesickness then, thinking of his family back in Upton County. He needed to get back there one of these days.

"This place is too small to run many cattle, and it's too rough to farm," said Baker. "So it's hard to make a livin' on."

"What are you going to do with it? You don't have any children to leave it to."

"Oh, I'll keep it, even if I go back to Texas. I got one niece, so I reckon I'll leave it to her someday. They ain't makin' any more land, Hewey. I figure one day this place will be worth a fortune."

Hewey didn't know about that. He'd heard about land back in Upton County bringing five dollars per acre, for ranchland at that. That seemed exorbitantly high to him. He didn't figure land could ever go higher. Nobody could afford to pay for it.

Hewey got that hair-on-end feeling again as he and Baker approached the cabin of the man who had held a shotgun on him.

"Fellow there won't be too hospitable if he recognizes me," he said to Baker. "Best not to slow down."

"You been makin' more friends, I guess," said Baker.

"He's just protectin' his family. He knows I had smallpox at the next cabin up the trail. He don't know his little girls carried us water and left it on the porch. When I come by here earlier he acted like he'd rather shoot me than have me on the place."

Baker laughed. "I'm not a doctor, but I do have some experience with this particular ailment. They say once the scabs fall off you can't make anyone sick. You're safe to be around now, Hewey."

Baker could see the relief wash over his friend's face. Hewey had never let much worry him, even when things might should have, but the thought of making someone else sick, especially a kid, had been weighing on his mind.

The two rode on, swapping well-rehearsed tales. Baker recounted episodes from his years as a lawman, all noted in a well-worn tally book he still carried. Some of Hewey's stories might have been true, too, but he'd told them all so often he wasn't quite certain which ones.

"This is it," Hewey told Baker when they rounded a bend and came even with the cabin where he had spent so much time.

"From your description, I figured it was," Baker replied. "A little run-down from age, just like my castle. It's sure seen better times, but then the Wilsons passed on several years ago, first her and then him."

"The who?" Hewey interrupted.

"The Wilsons."

"Well, I'll be damned," Hewey mumbled, mostly to himself.

"They had a boy when I knew 'em, called him Bobby. He'd be a grown man by now."

"And he'd call himself Bob Wilson," Hewey offered, shaking his head.

"Sure," Baker said in agreement. "What else?"

"I'll be damned," Hewey mumbled.

CHAPTER FOUR

Two days later Hewey and Baker rode into Durango about dinnertime and headed straight for the same café where Hewey had eaten breakfast the last time he was in town.

Hewey was not certain how long ago that had been. Three weeks, he guessed, but it seemed much longer.

The first person Hewey saw inside the café was his old friend Deputy Wiggins, who motioned them to join him at his table.

"Hanley, how have you been?" asked the deputy, shaking hands with each of them. Deputy Frank Wiggins and Hanley Baker had become friends the year before during the unpleasant business with Billy Joe Bradley, Clay Hawkins, and their partner, Jesse Sloan.

"Been good, Frank. Made the winter out at the cabin just fine. I was gettin' sort of lonesome, but in two days Hewey has talked enough to last me through this summer and next winter, too."

The same waitress who had served breakfast to Hewey and Wiggins weeks before brought coffee, and then a bowl of greasy chili and crackers to each of them. Hewey had been looking forward to something like fried chicken and maybe some biscuits and gravy, but he had dealt with surly waitresses before. He ate the chili.

"Chili's pretty good here," said the deputy, smiling at them. "It can be a little hard on the stomach, but it tastes good."

Both Hewey and Baker knew what he meant. They had each eaten enough greasy meals in cow camps and Ranger camps to understand.

When they were finished, Wiggins turned and gave Hewey a stern look. "Not long ago I told you to stay out of trouble. Then several days ago a posse limped through here headed home. They weren't much for conversation, but when I pressed them they did tell me they had a standoff at a cabin near here with a man named Calloway. I don't suppose that was you, was it?"

Hewey looked a little sheepish. "Story of my life. I was just mindin' my own business when that Pinkerton man and his posse started tryin' to arrest me for robbin' a bank. I told them I hadn't robbed any banks and that they'd have trouble arrestin' me. They could tell by lookin' at me that I'm an honest and truthful man, and I guess that was enough to suit them, so they let me go."

Both Wiggins and Baker stared at Hewey in silence for a few moments, then Baker just shook his head. "Was the Pinkerton man with them?" Baker asked Wiggins.

"No, this was just some local men that had joined the posse. They stuck it out longer than most posses, I guess, but these fellers had enough and were going home."

"Where was home?" Baker asked. "Where did this robbery happen?"

"Place way north of here called Green Ridge. Heard of it but never been there. They said this feller who robbed the bank shot it out with the bank owner on his way out of town."

Hewey snorted in disbelief. Baker was silent, thinking. Wiggins watched him, as it was apparent something was on the old Ranger's mind. "There is something wrong with this, but I can't figure what it is," Baker said finally. "Why was there a Pinkerton man in Green Ridge, Colorado? And why in the hell is the banker still out there with him, huntin' the bank robber? That doesn't make sense to me."

"Something smells funny to me, too," said Wiggins. "But

Green Ridge is a long way from here. Nobody broke any laws around here, and everybody involved has moved on, 'cept for Hewey here. I don't guess I'm involved."

"No, none of us are," said Baker, although the old lawman's tone said otherwise. "Something about it just doesn't sit right with me."

Hewey paid the check for everyone, and the men walked outside just as an electric streetcar slowly went past.

Wiggins hardly looked, but Hewey and Baker stared. "Would you look at that," said Baker.

"We better get out of here before progress swallows us up," replied Hewey.

※

They stocked up with supplies that would not spoil on the trail. They planned to keep themselves in fresh meat along the way. Hewey kept a sharp eye on the gray mule as they loaded the panniers on the pack saddle.

"You better not kick me again, you little son of a bitch," Hewey told the mule. He had nothing but patience for a horse or mule that was young or frightened, but he had little use for an older animal that fought out of spite.

They headed north out of Durango with no exact destination or timeline. Hewey thought he had seen mountains before, but as they traveled north the mountains became only grander.

They fed themselves with fish that were easily caught out of the numerous streams that came down out of the mountains. Deer and even elk were plentiful, but both men disliked shooting them when they could avoid it because too much of the meat spoiled before two men could eat it. Baker was familiar with the area, but Hewey was in awe of the clear mountain lakes they rode upon every day or two. This was a far cry from the desert country to which he was accustomed.

The mountains grew larger, and they followed a valley formed by mountains on each side. Baker told Hewey this was called the Animas River valley, and they followed it into the town of Silverton.

"We best be careful," Hewey advised his friend. "I got a bad history with towns called Silverton. You ever been to Silverton, up in the Texas Panhandle?"

"No, but I come close once during my Rangerin' days. We followed a horse thief all the way from down by Fort Worth. I bet we trailed that sucker three hundred miles before we lost him up in the Panhandle. He knew that country and ran to it just like the Comanches did thirty years ago. He sure went to a lot of trouble to steal two horses, the fool. He could've made a living easier working an honest job."

Baker looked over at Hewey. "What happened to you in Silverton to make you leery?"

"Me and Snort hired on at the JA, spent three months out with the wagon. When the spring works were done we drew our pay and drifted south, and the first place we come to was this little town of Silverton. You might find this hard to believe, Hanley, but in my younger days I would occasionally stray from the straight and narrow."

"You don't say," answered Baker.

"Well, me and Snort found us a saloon and got started sort of early in the day. We'd been out at the JA wagon for several months and hadn't tasted nothin' but water and coffee, so that whiskey sure was good. We were still at it early that evening, and I got to feelin' like I better find somethin' to eat or I was gonna be sick. Snort didn't want to quit drinkin', but I talked him into goin' to a little café down the road.

"Well, before we got to the café we come up on this fat man whipping a little boy with his belt, right in the street. Now, you know I like to mind my own business, but this seemed a mite excessive to me and Snort. So we told this feller he might like to ease up a little, and he told us he wasn't takin' orders from any cowhands."

As he often did, Hewey had the reins draped across Biscuit's neck. He could cue his mount with his legs just as well as his hands. This way his hands were free for rolling a cigarette or whatever else he needed to do. In this case that was for acting out his story.

"Me and Snort, we figured that was mighty impolite of this little feller and that maybe he needed a spankin' of his own. So, Snort just grabbed this feller and held his arms. He wasn't no match for Snort, being a soft town feller. Well, I took off my belt and went to whippin' him across the butt.

"I was swattin' him pretty hard, and this little town dude started cryin' and yellin' worse than the kid had been earlier, and here come all the locals. I thought they were gonna kill us right there, but this old sheriff showed up and kept them off us. I believe he sort of thought it was funny, but he still locked us up for the night."

Baker rode along, listening and wondering where in the world this windy tale could be headed.

"Turned out that fat man was the Baptist preacher in that little town, that's why everybody got so uptight." Hewey paused a moment for effect. "I've been a Methodist ever since."

Baker burst out laughing, but he wondered if it might be safer to go around Silverton, and maybe every other town they came to, so long as Hewey was with him.

❖

Against Baker's better judgement, they found a saloon downtown. The bar was made of rough pine, and there were no stools. Many of the tables and chairs showed patching, likely from one of the scuffles that so often occurred in saloons just like this one, no matter the town or place.

Gold miners filled the room, and there wasn't a cowboy to be found. Hewey was working on his second drink when he saw the Pinkerton man, Murphy, walk into the saloon, closely followed by the banker named Booker.

Hewey pointed them out to Baker, who watched them closely

from across the room. The newcomers walked to the bar and ordered their drinks, but Baker could tell right away that both were more interested in the crowd than their whiskeys.

Soon enough Murphy's eyes lit on Hewey, and he strode across the room to their table.

"Calloway, isn't it?" asked Murphy. Hewey didn't care for his manner any more than he had back at the cabin near Durango. "You wouldn't be up here to meet up with your partner, would you?"

Baker also did not care for the Pinkerton man's tone. "Hewey Calloway had nothing to do with this bank robbery. You have no evidence to suggest he did, which you know."

Obviously Murphy was not accustomed to being spoken to in such a manner. "Who in the hell are you?" he asked. "Perhaps you were in it also. I should have you both arrested on suspicion."

"You would have a hard time arrestin' me, friend," replied Baker, rising to his feet. "I suggest you move on."

Murphy looked Baker up and down, lingering for a moment on the Colt on his hip. Murphy smiled at Baker, then at Hewey, and the expression on his face gave Hewey the chills. Murphy was not the least bit intimidated.

"Good evening, gentlemen," Murphy said with a smirk.

Hewey watched him speak briefly with the banker, then the two left. "I told you, Hanley. Towns called Silverton are bad luck."

They spent the night under a tree near the livery stable, where they had stashed their horses and mule for the night. The next morning they were at one of the local cafés when it opened, and they left town as quickly as possible. They didn't see Murphy again, but both were ready to put the town behind them after replenishing their food supplies.

※

Aside from when they passed through towns or populated areas, Baker turned the little gray mule loose and it followed along, carrying the pack saddle. Hewey began to develop an appreciation for the mule, although he never developed much trust or affection. The way the mule looked at him he figured the feeling was mutual.

They fell into a routine of traveling fairly steadily most of the day, unless they found something interesting that warranted a detour or stop. They usually camped by midafternoon, typically along one of the rivers, streams, or lakes that were so common. They had no schedule, and the early camping allowed them to fish and prepare their supper in the daylight hours.

Baker often bathed in these mountain waters, and Hewey stepped up his bathing schedule to every few days or so. He never grew accustomed to the water temperature, though.

"Dammit, Hanley," he said one afternoon as he was easing into a shallow stream in only his long underwear. It always took Hewey several minutes to lower himself into the cold water. "It's the middle of summer. It's hot during the day. How in the hell is this water so cold? In Texas the rivers have the sense to warm up in the summertime."

There was still snow on many of the higher peaks, and Baker told Hewey that he had seen it snow in July above the tree line. Hewey pointed out that West Texas rarely sees snow even in January.

One evening Baker sat poking the campfire with a skinny piece of green pine. He told Hewey that his brother lived a few days' ride northwest of there, and his niece lived in southern Wyoming. "I'd like to go through there and see them for a few days," Baker said. "I haven't seen my niece in several years. She's a schoolteacher at a little town up there. I can't get this close without going by there."

Hewey was silent a moment. Family visits had often proved uncomfortable for him, and he was not too sure he wanted to go visit a family that wasn't even his. He sat thinking of the sharp tongues on several of the women he knew, such as his sister-in-law, Eve, or his friend Alvin Lawdermilk's mother-in-law. Those two always targeted Hewey unfairly, in his opinion.

The last time he was at Walter and Eve's place, she had even told him to leave and not come back. He wondered if Baker might have some female kinfolks who might like to lecture him about his footloose ways.

Hewey finally looked up at Baker, who wasn't a bit surprised at Hewey's decision. "You know, I think I might just ease along by myself and meet up with you on the trail somewhere. It's nothin' against your family. I just don't have a good history of gettin' along with domestic-thinkin' women."

"That's fine with me, Hewey. You'd like my niece, though. She takes after her daddy. But my sister-in-law, she'd pick you apart after a day or two, I'm afraid. She don't hold with wanderin' cowboys that don't attend church regular. She'll be after me soon enough for not ever marrying."

The next morning they divvied up their groceries as best they could. Baker offered to send the mule with Hewey but received only a disgusted snort in response. They made plans to meet up in southern Wyoming at Laramie. Baker's niece lived near there at a small town called Harmony.

"I'll see you in two weeks at Laramie," Baker said, hoping his friend would be punctual, although it seemed doubtful.

Hewey shook Baker's hand. "I'll be there."

"Stay out of trouble, Hewey," Baker told him.

Hewey grinned. "Why's everybody always tellin' me that?"

Baker left camp at a trot, angling a little west of north. Hewey, with nowhere in particular to be, eased out in a walk, still headed north, and enjoying the warm early-morning sunshine that had broken clear of the peaks to the east.

CHAPTER FIVE

Hewey took his time, which he was prone to do when he had no particular place to be at the moment. He followed roads or wagon trails when it suited him, but just as often he would head off through the trees on a lark.

He changed course often when something piqued his interest, and it was not difficult to arouse his curiosity. He spent half of one day picking his way up the side of a mountain when he saw a herd of animals he could not identify.

The terrain eventually became too steep and rocky for Biscuit, so Hewey staked the horse on a small patch of green grass and continued on foot. He had never been much for walking and would have bowed out if he had been told to climb a mountain afoot, but this was different since it was his own idea. The animals were above him, but Hewey kept in the trees for cover as he slowly made his way through the rocks. After an hour of treacherous and painful climbing, he poked his head above a rock outcropping and looked upon a herd of sheep, although these were unlike any sheep he had ever seen.

Hewey had spent much of life taking care of cattle, so he counted these without even realizing he was doing it.

There were seventeen adult sheep and eleven lambs, that he could see at least. Hewey could spot the rams due to their massive horns.

He thought back over the years to a tale around a campfire

at a wagon out in the Big Bend country. He could not remember the old cowboy's name, but he could picture his face. One night this old-timer told them about bighorn sheep he had seen years earlier in New Mexico and Colorado. It had seemed unreal to Hewey at the time, wild sheep living at the tops of mountains, but here they were, sunning on the side of a mountain not fifty yards from him.

Hewey had been out of fresh meat for a day, and he had taken his carbine from his saddle and carried it with him up the mountain. He looked at the sheep above, and they were a wonder to him. He decided he could make do with what provisions he had in his saddlebags.

He settled into a more comfortable position against the rock, careful not to spook the sheep, and just sat and watched. Soon the sheep stood and began to graze lazily.

Two rams hooked each other with their horns, but their hearts were not in it just then. The lambs nursed, aggressively butting their mothers' udders until the frustrated ewes walked away.

Hewey watched until the sheep all went out of sight behind a cluster of rocks that jutted from the side of the mountain. He sat another few minutes, enjoying himself and soaking in the moment. Many times over the years he had been lectured for his footloose ways. Most of those giving the lectures were tied down, whether it be to a farm like his brother, Walter, or a big ranch like old C. C. Tarpley, or even to their wives and families. They didn't know what they were missing, Hewey concluded. He wouldn't trade places with any of them.

❖

A couple days later he hit an established road that wound through the mountains, seemingly heading mostly east or west. Hewey turned east. The road was made of dirt and rock, but care had been taken in places to blast a narrow roadway from the side of the mountain when there was no easier path. He was impressed but saddened in a way. Too much progress, he mused.

The owner of a small general store where Hewey stopped to replenish his supplies told him the road would hit Denver in another hundred and fifty miles or so. Hewey had never seen Denver but did not feel a pull toward the place. He liked to visit a town every once in a while, but from what the storekeeper told him Denver would be too big for his tastes.

Hewey was sitting at the store counter eating a bowl of stew with some crackers on the side. There wasn't a café for several miles, so the storekeeper kept a pot of stew or chili warm for any hungry travelers who stopped in his store. The meat was elk, he said, and Hewey thought it was delicious. The old man told him it was ten cents for as much as he could hold but began to get nervous when Hewey asked for a third bowl of stew and more crackers.

The storekeeper had an accent Hewey could not identify and spoke in a proper manner that Hewey had rarely heard.

He was a pleasant old man with brown skin, a neat gray mustache, and a fortunate amount of gray hair. He seemed to enjoy Hewey's company, and Hewey was himself hungry for conversation.

"They say there are over a hundred thousand people living in Denver now," said the old storekeeper sadly. His daughter lived there, and between the distance and his distrust of big cities he did not see her or his grandchildren as much as he would like. He held a grudge against Denver for it.

"They have automobiles, I reckon," Hewey said between bites.

"Hundreds now, I've heard." The storekeeper rubbed his forehead. The thought gave him a headache. His buggy horse had nearly had a runaway the last time he and his wife went to visit their grandchildren. His horse did not care for automobiles any more than he did.

"Those contraptions won't last," said Hewey. "I've seen a bunch of 'em. Somebody is always workin' on 'em or fixin' a flat tire. Give it a few years."

"I hope you're right, my young friend, but I'm not certain.

These cities are different places than people like you and I know. They have buildings ten stories tall, and many of them have electricity and some even have running water. But there are so many people."

The man shook his head, feeling sad for his grandchildren who were growing up in that hell, and for himself for having to witness it.

"My grandkids, they won't know what the world is all about," he mused. "All they'll know is that place."

From outside came a clattering noise that slowly grew louder. Hewey knew from his limited experience it was an automobile.

The storekeeper frowned even more. "Once or twice a day they stop, but they rarely buy much. They're in too much of a hurry."

Hewey had finished his meal, and out of curiosity they both stepped outside. A middle-aged man wearing a derby hat and driving goggles was stepping out of the small black automobile. A slightly younger woman sat staring forward, refusing to look at the driver, or maybe at Hewey and the storekeeper. Hewey wasn't certain which it was.

"Do you sell gasoline?" asked the man, removing a pair of thin leather gloves. Hewey had seen automobile drivers wearing these gloves but had never understood why. The afternoon was pleasantly warm.

"I am sorry, sir. I do not sell petrol. I suppose I should begin."

"Dammit! How far is it to a store that does sell it?" Hewey didn't like the man's tone, and it only seemed to sadden the storekeeper.

"I believe Mr. McCormick has begun to carry petrol at his store," the storekeeper said helpfully. "It is only four miles farther, along this same road."

The automobile driver turned without a word and stomped to his vehicle. "I believe we have enough to make it, Laura. These Podunk stores need to get with the times. It's unbelievable!"

Laura continued to frown and stare forward. Hewey took a step toward the man, but the old storekeeper reached out and touched him on the arm, gently. When Hewey looked over, the man shook his head sadly then beckoned Hewey to follow him inside.

"It is not worth it, my friend," he said quietly. "The world is changing. I fear for the younger generations, if this is where we are headed."

Hewey stocked up on coffee, bacon, flour, salt, and a few other essentials, buying more than he could easily carry because he liked the old storekeeper. He even bought some canned fruit, a treat he rarely purchased because it was difficult to carry. In the end he had more than would fit in his saddlebags, so the storekeeper placed the rest in a flour sack that Hewey tied to his saddle horn.

"I thank you, my friend, both for the business and for the conversation," said the old man.

"My pleasure, sir. Don't you fret too much about these automobiles and all this so called progress. Everythin' will get back right before you know it."

The old man sat on the edge of his porch and stared sadly as Hewey rode away. He was not as optimistic.

✦

Hewey heard the travelers before he saw them, or at least he heard the man.

"Goddamit!" came the harsh voice from ahead. Hewey topped a small rise and below him saw the car stuck in a small mudhole left by one of the summer showers that were so prevalent. The man was attempting to dig in front of his tires but seemed unaccustomed to manual labor and unfamiliar with his tool. The mud was apparently sticky, and he was having trouble walking in it.

Hewey and Biscuit eased down the hill and stopped just outside the mudhole. The man, bent over next to a front tire, did not notice them immediately. Laura was still staring forward in silence.

Hewey rolled a cigarette, and when he struck a match the

man looked around. "Hey, cowboy, you best help me or ride along. Don't just sit there and watch."

"Sounds good to me, mister." Hewey nudged Biscuit into a walk. They crossed the mudhole and continued east.

"Wait! Wait! There's no need for that," said the man, trying to walk through the mud toward Hewey. His feet kept getting stuck. "I'll give you a dollar if you'll just help me get out of here."

Hewey slowly turned Biscuit and walked back toward the man. "I ought to leave you here, mister, but I'm going to help you since you have that lady there with you. I don't want your money. I want somethin' else."

The man looked impatient and angry. Laura stared forward.

"The next time you drive that contraption through here, I want you to stop at that store back yonder, the one you stopped at earlier. I want you to give that old man two dollars, and then I want you to tell him you're sorry for acting like a jackass. Deal?"

The man seethed. No one spoke to him like this in the office. However, he had never been one for physical confrontation. He also knew he was in a bind.

"Deal," he hissed, although he had no intention of apologizing to some foreigner who ran a Podunk store out in the hills.

Hewey shook out his rope and pitched the loop to the man. "Put that around that piece on the front, whatever it's called."

"That would be the bumper," said the man contemptuously, but he slid the loop over the end of the metal bumper.

"Turn on that contraption so you can help. I don't want to hurt my horse over no damn automobile."

It took several minutes for the man to crank the vehicle and get behind the wheel. He gave it some gas and Biscuit leaned into the rope, and the car popped free.

Hewey stopped as soon as the rear wheels cleared the mud, and the man nearly ran the car over Biscuit. Hewey glared at him, and the man remained in the car.

"All right, cowboy. Unhitch your rope so we can be on our way."

"Mister, *you* unhitch my rope or I'll drag that damn contraption right back in the mud."

He reined Biscuit toward the mud, and the man gave in just as the rope got tight.

"Hold on, hold on," he said, getting out of the car.

He slid the loop of Hewey's rope off the bumper and dropped it. He turned without appreciation and started for the vehicle.

"You cowboys need to learn your place," he said. "Your time is up and you just don't know it."

The man turned to open his door just as Biscuit knocked into him, side-passing down the side of the car. The collision did not knock down the man, but it did force him to stumble toward the rear of the car. Biscuit kept moving sideways, pushing the man.

"Whoa, Biscuit, whoa!" Hewey shouted. "What's come over you? Whoa!"

Biscuit didn't whoa, since Hewey was nudging him in the rib cage with his right spur and wasn't even tightening the reins. He was flailing his arms dramatically, but it was all for show. They picked up speed, with Biscuit pushing the man ahead of him.

The man lost his balance when his feet hit the mud, and he landed with a splash. When he tried to push himself up the suction caught one of his leather driving gloves and he came up without it. He tried to cuss Hewey, but his mouth was full of grit.

"I apologize, ma'am," Hewey said. "These horses are hard to control sometimes. Might be I need to trade him in for an automobile."

He tipped his hat toward Laura, who still stared forward. Hewey thought he saw her mouth twitch in a small smile, but he wasn't sure. He turned Biscuit and hit a trot down the road, whistling a cheerful tune.

CHAPTER SIX

Two days later Hewey rode into a town that made up for its small size with activity. It was late afternoon, and the one street was bustling. There were only a handful of businesses in town, running down the main road through town, with one residential section to the east. To the west of the main thoroughfare was the biggest collection of tents Hewey had ever seen. He had once seen a photo hanging on the wall in a café of hundreds of white military tents set up somewhere on the frontier, and this reminded him of that although without the order. Rough trails wound through the tents with no particular pattern that Hewey could spot. He sat on Biscuit for several minutes, staring and wondering.

It was late enough in the day that Hewey knew he would end up staying the night, whether he planned on it or not, so he left Biscuit at the livery stable. The brown gelding had spent many an hour tied in front of saloons, but when he had the forethought Hewey preferred to leave him in a pen at the livery stable with some hay and a few oats.

There were only two horses tied outside the saloon, but the place was practically full. Either everyone else was being nice to their horses or these fellows all walked, he thought. He was a long way from Texas.

Men had been coming and going all afternoon, and no one

paid any attention to Hewey when he entered the saloon. He picked out an unclaimed space at the near end of the bar, ordered a whiskey, and slid a coin out ahead of him to pay for it.

"Who lives in all them tents out there?" Hewey asked the bartender when the man reached for the coin. The bartender was a middle-aged, heavyset man who did not act particularly friendly or talkative. He gave Hewey an aggravated look. He didn't have time for idle conversation.

"Miners." The bartender nodded his head toward the crowd of working men that filled the saloon. He walked away as if that were explanation enough.

Idly scanning his fellow patrons, Hewey saw a face that he had never expected to see again. When his glass came, he picked it up and worked his way down the bar, slipping in beside the man he had eyed from half a room away.

"What say you and me go sit somewhere away from all these people?" he asked quietly.

The familiar stranger turned quickly, looked Hewey in the face, and blanched visibly, his eyes rapidly glancing around the room as if searching for an escape route.

"I don't mean you any trouble; just have a few questions I'd like to hear some answers to," Hewey continued.

He pointed out an empty table along the far wall, and the two men worked their way to it. Hewey sat across the small table from the other man, whose gaze was focused on the glass of whiskey in his hands. He turned the glass several times.

"Did you trail me all the way up here?" the man asked nervously.

"Not even close," Hewey said. "It was a real surprise to walk in here and spot you. I don't know what you're callin' yourself these days, but I doubt it's Bob Wilson, and it don't matter anyhow. Didn't want to give anything away calling you by the wrong name, though. It was pretty clear back at the cabin that you were sittin' on some secrets, but it wasn't any of my business, so I let it go.

"But then a few days after you pulled out a posse showed up lookin' for a man who'd robbed a bank awhile back. That answered some of my questions and raised some others."

Hewey finished his drink and wished for another. Bob Wilson had forgotten his.

"First off, why you would stay around that cabin and tend to me when you had to know that the dogs were on your scent?"

"I owed you," Bob Wilson answered, "and I couldn't go off and leave a sick man who got that way tending to me when I was sick myself."

Hewey gave him a long look. "A real outlaw would have done it without hesitatin' for a minute."

"Like I said, I owed you."

"And I get the feelin' you ain't much of a real outlaw."

"No, Mr. Calloway, I'm not," Wilson said, "but I might as well be now. They've got me down as robbing that bank, when all I did was overhear the real robbers."

"Talk in town was that you shot it out with the bank owner as you escaped with your saddlebags bulging."

"I never fired a shot," Wilson countered, "just hung as low as I could over my saddle as I left town, and the only bulges in my saddlebags were from what I'd already put in there, a few nuggets of my own and some folding money. This is going to sound funny under the circumstances, but I thought the safest place for something like that was in a bank's vault, and that's why I was there in the first place."

"What do you plan to do next?" Wilson asked quietly.

"I don't have any real plans," Hewey replied.

"There's bound to be a sizeable reward for a sure-enough bank robber."

"You've just told me you're no bank robber," Hewey continued.

"And you're taking me at my word?"

"That and the fact that you hung around when you should have run."

"You're a strange man, Mr. Calloway."

"Hewey. It's just Hewey."

"Still, there's easy money to be made," Wilson answered.

"I hear there's money to be made runnin' hogs, too," Hewey said with a grin, "but I've never felt the itch to do it. I don't know about a reward, anyway. I don't read many newspapers. They're mostly full of stories about things that happened to people I don't know in places I've never heard of. No, we were even when you left the cabin, maybe better'n even for me, considerin' that you stayed when most men in your kind of a pickle would've ridden on as soon as they could stay in the saddle."

"Like I said, I couldn't leave you there to die."

"And like *I* said, that's what separates you from the outlaws," Hewey answered. "Now, I'll buy another round or two of drinks, and after that we can go our own ways. If I run into you again, though, I may turn you in just to stop trippin' over you."

That got a laugh out of Wilson, the first time Hewey could recall hearing such a sound out of him. The young man relaxed noticeably.

"I had a sure-enough sinking spell when you sidled up beside me at the bar, but now I'm glad we bumped into each other," Wilson said, a look of relief on his face. "It gets lonesome, having a story to get off my chest and not being able to tell anybody."

"I couldn't have held it as long as you have," Hewey admitted, "but then, I'm a shade more talkative."

He had barely finished saying that when a gunshot roared behind him. It was almost deafening, but Hewey could still hear the bullet whiz past his right ear, so close it picked up a trace of week-old whiskers. He and Wilson were under the table in an instant.

The second shot ricocheted off the table and broke the window behind them. Glancing at each other and nodding simultaneously, he and Wilson each grabbed a table leg and jerked the whole thing over in front of them for a shield. By then miners, bankers, and barflies were scattering.

"Goddamn you, cowboy!" a voice bellowed with a distinct slur. "You leave my wife the hell alone!"

The third bullet struck the heavy tabletop but did not penetrate. Hewey felt the table move from the impact.

"I'll see to it you never make eyes at her again!" The voice was closer that time.

Hewey and Wilson both looked at each other with their own eyes wide.

"I swear, I never," Wilson blurted.

"Hell, I just got to town," Hewey whispered.

Just then came a short series of unusual sounds—the first a dull crack quickly followed by a groan and then a heavier thud.

"You boys can come out now," said another voice.

Hewey and Wilson carefully peeked around opposite sides of the table. There stood the heavyset bartender wearing an apron and holding a short wooden club.

On the floor at the bartender's feet lay an average-sized man, ragged-looking and unkempt. A six-shooter was near his right hand.

Almost in unison, Hewey and Bob Wilson began talking over each other, both so nervous they did not realize they were doing it. They were both assuring and swearing they never messed with the man's wife.

"No need," the bartender replied. "His wife ran off with a cowboy a couple of months ago. Ever since then, about once a week he gets liquored up and on the prod. Usually he just wants to fight. It just happened that this time he decided to kill one of you."

"Which one of us, you reckon?" Hewey asked, clearly remembering the bullet that came so close to his ear.

"Who knows?" answered the bartender. "He probably didn't even know himself. What's it matter?"

"Well, it would've mattered if he'd been a better shot," Hewey said.

"Couple of the boys will drag him out on the porch and mind him until the city marshal shows up to claim him for a day or two," the bartender said. "My apologies for the ruckus. He's not supposed to set foot in this place, but somehow he slipped in unnoticed. I was busy and not lookin' close. Your next round is on the house, to make up for the ones you had to spill."

"If you've got about half a bottle back yonder, why don't you just bring the whole thing?" Hewey said. "I'd even be happy with the cheap stuff."

The bartender asked a couple regular customers to drag the unconscious man outside, and then he went along the walls, lighting the kerosene lanterns that hung every few feet.

Hewey watched, curious since there were already electric lights burning, if dimly. He watched until the bartender was done. A few minutes later all the electric lights blinked out.

Hewey called out to bartender, "What was that all about?"

"The sawmill generates the electricity here in town," the man explained, "and when the mill shuts down at night, the lights go out. You'd best be ready, or you'll be sitting in the dark. At least they do it at the same time every night."

"Well, I'll be damned," Hewey said.

"The modern world will not be denied," Wilson observed.

※

The half-bottle proved to be too much for them. Age had somewhat tempered Hewey's desire for serious drinking. He could still do it from time to time, but the mood had to be right, and it was not just then. As likeable as Wilson was, the kid was just too nervous to be a lot of fun, Hewey thought to himself. He couldn't blame him, though. He figured he would be jumpy, too, if he were wanted for bank robbery.

When they left the saloon Hewey carried the whiskey bottle with him. He had paid for it and wasn't about to leave it behind.

"I might find some traveler down the road in need of medicine," he explained to Wilson, who only raised his eyebrows in response.

They walked two doors down to a café, the sort of place that did not serve anything fancy but made up for it with good food in generous portions. It was Hewey's kind of place.

They each ordered the daily special, a steak with fried potatoes, corn on the cob, biscuits, and coffee. Hewey asked for an extra biscuit. He received a frown from the gray-haired waitress but did get the biscuit. It had been a long time since Hewey had eaten corn on the cob. He figured someone must have a big garden nearby.

"If I lived in a town where I could eat like this every day I'd be fat as a hog," Hewey said halfway through the meal.

He looked at Wilson. "You don't look like you been eatin' too much yourself."

Wilson had been thin the last Hewey saw of him, which was understandable considering his recent bout with smallpox. But he didn't appear to have gained even a pound of flesh since.

"Mostly I've been stayin' out of towns. I keep thinkin' I'm going to turn around and see somebody that's huntin' me. I'd rather stay out and eat my own cookin' than risk it. The only reason I was in that saloon was I had got so lonesome bein' by myself for so long. But when I got in there I was too scared to talk to anyone."

"What are you plannin'?" Hewey asked. "You can't run forever."

"I don't know, Mr. Calloway. I think about it all the time but I don't come up with any good ideas. I don't have any kin or anywhere to go."

"What happened to your folks? I know you grew up in that cabin where I found you."

Wilson gave him a quizzical look but said, "Ma died when I was thirteen. She'd been sick for a while. Then Pa died about three years later, all of a sudden one day. It was his heart, the doctor in town told me later. I been on my own since."

Hewey had lost both his parents at a young age, and he and his brother, Walter, had faced some hard times afterward. He knew what Wilson had faced and felt for him.

"I own the farm there, but now I don't know if I can ever go back. I shouldn't have led that posse there, but I was scared and didn't know what else to do. That place is not hardly big enough to make a good living, but it's a start. If I can get shut of all this."

Hewey studied the young man briefly. "I ain't got you figured just yet. You look sorta like a cowpuncher, but you mentioned some gold nuggets."

Wilson smiled. "All I ever really wanted to be was a cowboy, but I've spent some time in the mines when I'd get tired of bein' broke. Then I'd get sick of the mines and get me a ranch job. Then I'd get to feelin' poor and go back to the mines.

"I'd been on the Rocker C on the other side of the divide for about a year, then we heard about the gold strike near Green Ridge. A couple of us drew our wages and headed out there. I was a miner for about a month that time, I reckon.

"Now I'd just like to go back to being a cowboy," Wilson said sadly. "Or something else simple and honest."

Wilson had not finished his supper and had begun to pick at it absentmindedly. He was young and thin, but the talk of his current situation had ruined his appetite. Hewey could see the cloud of worry come over the young man.

"I been sort of staying close, hopin' they would catch the real bank robbers. If I leave out for Mexico or someplace far, I might never hear. I could be a free man and not know it. I get a newspaper when I can, prayin' to read they've caught someone and I'm in the clear. Hasn't happened yet though."

"What if you found a lawman you could trust and turned yourself in?"

"I thought about that a lot, but what if they don't believe me? That posse sure thought it was me. You said there's a Pinkerton man trailing me. I seen a man hang once, and up until they pulled that handle he screamed that he was innocent. Didn't nobody believe him. I'm scared they won't listen and will hang me just the same."

Hewey thought about that for a moment. He could see Wilson's point and wasn't sure what he would do in the same situation. "I wish Hanley Baker was here. I bet he'd know what to do."

"Who's that? The name sounds sort of familiar," asked Wilson.

"He's an old Texas Ranger and a friend of mine. He's supposed to be retired, but that don't suit him. I'm supposed to meet him in a few days. You ought to come with me, see what he thinks."

"I appreciate the offer, Mr. Calloway. I really do. But I think I'll just head out on my own and stay scarce. No offense to your friend, but he was a Ranger. What if he just takes me in?"

"Hanley wouldn't do that." Still, Hewey could understand Wilson's hesitance. He'd had a few run-ins with bad lawmen himself. "Tell you what, you think about it. I don't know how, but I bet Hanley can help you. I'm supposed to meet him in nine or ten days in Laramie, Wyoming. I understand if you don't want to ride with me, but if you change your mind, meet me there and we'll see what Hanley thinks."

"I thank you, Mr. Calloway, and I will think about it." Wilson left enough money on the table for them both, stood, and walked out. Hewey sat alone for a few minutes. He liked the boy and wished he could do something to help.

Hewey slept in his bedroll under a tree outside the livery stable. He had money for a room at the small hotel, but despite his carefree attitude toward money, he just did not see any point wasting it on something so frivolous.

The next morning he stowed his bedroll with his saddle, fed Biscuit, and walked the short distance to the same café where he had eaten the night before. The same gray-haired waitress brought him a cup of coffee. Hewey ordered ham and eggs with potatoes and biscuits.

"Ma'am, reckon I could get an extra biscuit, please?" Hewey smiled at her as nicely as he could. The gray-haired waitress turned and walked away with no response whatsoever. She didn't say a word when she brought his breakfast, either, but there were three biscuits on his plate.

After breakfast Hewey splurged a little, in his opinion, on a haircut and shave, both of which he was in serious need of. He considered a hot bath, which was offered in the back room, but decided the next creek or lake would do just fine. He didn't want too many luxuries to make him soft.

He saddled Biscuit and found a general store where he intended to buy some new socks and a shirt. His socks had hit the point where no seamstress could help them, and his shirt was thin enough he felt like the sun was burning him through it.

He walked into the store just as a conversation began at the counter. A pretty black-haired lady of perhaps thirty years stood near the counter with two frightened boys that Hewey figured were not yet five years old. The woman wore a faded purple dress that looked as if it had been bright and pretty many years earlier. The boys wore homemade pants and shirts, and the younger boy's clothes had likely belonged to the older brother first. Neither wore shoes, but then again it was summertime and many boys didn't wear their shoes.

Behind the counter was a tall, thin man with a bald head and a hawk nose.

"I told you last time that I couldn't give any more credit. I'm sorry, but I meant it," the man said firmly.

"Please, Mr. Voight, my children are hungry. When José is well we will pay you back. You know this." The woman had a strong Mexican accent and looked as if she was about to burst into tears.

"I'm sorry, Martina. I really am. Your account has a balance of ten dollars. That is our maximum. It's the policy."

"But you are the owner. The policy, it is yours. You have the power to change it."

The thin man had no response for this. The pair stared at each for a moment, neither speaking. The woman sighed and looked down at the two boys. "Lo siento, niños. Vamonos."

Hewey had stopped just inside the door, listening to the conversation, and when the family came his way he stepped over and held the door open for them. The woman looked at him, silent tears running down her face, and quietly said "Gracias." The two little boys, following just behind, each repeated their mother as they passed by.

Hewey thought for a second, looked at the thin man behind the counter, and followed the trio outside. The boys reminded him of his own nephews, Cotton and Tommy. He had spent a winter with them when they were about the age of these boys. He'd been there on the pretense of helping Walter build a barn and a few other things around the place, but Hewey stayed mostly because he enjoyed the company of his young nephews. He'd always had a soft spot for kids.

"Ma'am," Hewey called gently to the retreating lady, who turned and met his eyes, tears still trickling down her face.

"Do you need some help, ma'am?"

"Gracias, señor, but we are fine." She motioned to the boys to follow, but they hesitated, staring at Hewey.

"Muévete!" The boys jumped into motion, familiar with her tone and its consequences.

"Hold on, ma'am." Hewey trotted several steps to get in front of the lady, although he gave her plenty of space. He was also familiar with that tone. The lady stopped, but her expression showed more defiance than patience.

"I can tell you're in some sort of jam, and it's none of my business. I ain't askin' what's goin' on. But if you need a little help feedin' these boys, I'd sure be glad to do what I can. I don't want to see these little boys go off hungry, if that's what's happenin'."

The lady was silent, looking at Hewey and obviously thinking about her situation. Suddenly she turned and sat on the edge of the wooden porch and put her head in her hands. The boys and Hewey all looked at each other, none certain what to do. The older boy reached over and put his hand on his mother's shoulder. She reached back and placed her hand over his but didn't turn.

Hewey had never understood women, and his first instinct when emotions ran high was to flee, which he thought about doing then. He likely would have, had it not been for the small boys standing there, not knowing any more than he did how to help their mother. Hewey stepped off the porch and squatted on his heels in front of the lady.

"Ma'am, I'd be happy to buy some groceries for these boys, if that would help you," he said.

The woman uncovered her face. Tears still ran down her cheeks. "Dos meses, two months ago, my husband broke his leg. He works for a man dragging the trees down to the sawmill." She nodded her head in the direction of what Hewey assumed was the sawmill.

"The mules that day, I don't know how to say. Ellas no eran mansitas."

"Gentle," Hewey said helpfully. "The mules weren't gentle."

"The mules, they tried to run and the logs fell. They hit my husband. Aquí." She pointed to her lower leg. "So for two months he cannot work. We had some money saved, but it's gone now. I help in the hotel when it's busy, but it is not enough."

The storekeeper had come outside. He stood just outside his door, listening. Hewey looked up at the thin man, who nodded back as if confirming the woman's story.

"I gave them more credit than I've ever allowed someone before," he said plaintively. "They're good people, but it's all I could do." He turned and walked back inside.

"How long before your husband can work again?"

"No sé, maybe one more month." She shrugged her shoulders.

Hewey felt down in his pocket, trying to calculate how much money he had. He had come out of the winter and early spring with nearly all his wages, since there had not been much opportunity to spend them. He had left the ranch with almost $150 in his pocket, but that was supposed to last to Canada and back.

"Hell, easy come, easy go," he said to himself.

"¿Cómo?" asked the lady.

"Nothin', ma'am." He dug through his pockets, then walked to his horse and dug around in the bottom of his saddlebags. He began counting out the money he found. The boys stared at him with big eyes.

"You boys hungry?" Hewey had an idea. He went back to his saddlebags and dug out a can of peaches and the primitive can opener he carried. The opener was difficult to use, but it had saved plenty of broken knife blades. He opened the can and handed it to the younger boy.

"Use your fingers. I won't tell your mother." He winked at the boys. "That's all I have, so share with your brother."

The boys began pulling the peach wedges out of the can and eating them slowly, relishing the treat. Fruit was a novelty, no matter one's economic situation.

Hewey returned to counting his money, laying it out in piles on the edge of the porch. He ended up with $103 and some change. He counted out half of it, leaving the other half lying on the porch.

The boys had finished the peaches, and the youngest was drinking the remaining juice from the can. Hewey smiled, watching. He looked down at the money in his hand. He counted out five dollars, shoved it in his pocket, and placed the rest on top of the stack he had left on the porch.

"This is a gift for them boys. I've been hurt before myself and probably will be again someday. This ought to get you by 'til your husband is well. Just tell him to be careful about them fool mules."

Before she could answer, Hewey turned and headed for Biscuit. He had made it one step when he was hit from behind by both boys, who grabbed his legs and were hugging them. The woman was again crying, but this time some quiet sobs escaped her. Hewey pulled the boys loose and squatted down in front of them.

"What are your names?"

The older one was Enrique, he learned.

"My name is Joe. I'm three," said the younger brother, holding up three fingers.

Hewey held out his hand, and they each shook it. "I'm Hewey Calloway. Nice to meet you.

"You boys, you do what you can to help your ma and your

pa right now, okay? Your pa's leg will be well soon enough, and things will be better. But you help out your folks, all right?"

The older boy nodded his head. The younger one grinned and said, "Yes, sir."

"You boys want to be cowboys when you grow up?"

Both boys nodded, the smaller with more enthusiasm.

"Get your pa to teach you. I'm sure he can. Then when you're old enough you can come work with me." This time he winked at their mother. "We'll hire on at the biggest ranch we can find. We'll go down to Texas, or maybe out to Arizona. I hear there are outfits out there where the horses are wild, the cattle are wilder, and the cowpunchers are the wildest of them all. How does that sound?"

The boys' eyes were wide, but they were both smiling. Hewey felt like they might not have smiled enough lately. He stood and patted them each on the head. The woman stood still. "Gracias, señor," she said quietly. Hewey nodded to her, untied Biscuit, and tightened his cinch. He grabbed the saddle horn with both hands, stuck his left foot in the stirrup, and stepped on.

The boys had gone to their mother's side. Hewey looked down at them and grinned, then turned and trotted out of town.

"Best part of the trip so far, Biscuit," he said to the brown horse. "Best part."

CHAPTER SEVEN

Hanley Baker settled his saddle lightly but firmly on the big bay, tightened the cinch, then added his bedroll and gave his niece a hug. Her real name was Susan, but her parents had begun calling her Daisy as a toddler. The name had stuck.

She was a small woman, slim and not very tall, but very pretty with long brown hair and brown eyes. She was still unmarried at twenty-two.

Daisy was a schoolteacher in the little town of Harmony, Wyoming. The school provided its only teacher with a small house that sat just behind the schoolhouse. Daisy had been there three years and had reportedly ran off several eligible young suitors. Her marital status did not trouble her uncle much, but it had begun to seriously concern her parents and some of the local ladies.

"I wish you would stay longer, Uncle Hanley," said Daisy. "I have enjoyed the family stories."

"I have, too," Baker said. "But you know me. I can't stay more than a few days before I get the itch to move on. It's left over from my Ranger days. But I'll be back again."

"See that you do," said his niece, then hugged him again.

"I'll tell you what," Baker said, relenting. "One more story, and it'll have to hold you for a while. Your daddy was a double handful sometimes. In fact, he kept us on our toes most of the time. Our papa would run out of patience with him pretty often.

"One day when I was still just a big ol' kid, I came in from a cow hunt to find your daddy tied to a tree out by the barn. Papa said it was the only way he could get anything done. Your daddy was just a kid, not even ten years old. Papa did it because he was afraid your daddy was gonna hurt himself, because he was so reckless.

"But your daddy didn't see it that way. He was none too happy about it, cussin' a blue streak and gettin' most of the words wrong.

"I couldn't even stay long enough to tend to my horse and find somethin' to eat myself because I'd have had both of 'em mad at me. I had to get out of earshot before I broke out laughin'. Killed most of the day hidin' out in the brush just to stay away from them.

"Your grandmother was gone somewhere, maybe to see her folks. I don't remember. But she'd have never stood for any of that. She'd have killed Papa for tying up her little boy, and she'd have whipped Jim for cussin' like that, and probably for whatever he done to get tied up in the first place."

Daisy broke into a fit of laughter, picturing her serious father behaving so poorly in his youth. To his own children he had always pretended to have been a saint during his own childhood.

"I'll have to ask him about this, next time I'm down there," Daisy said to her uncle, still giggling.

"Go ahead, but he won't be happy with me for tellin' it. Now I really do have to go. There's a footloose cowboy out there somewhere in need of guidance, and I'm the best chance he's got."

"How will you find him?"

"Oh, we're supposed to meet in Laramie in a couple days, if Hewey ain't forgot about it."

"I have a feeling you may both need each other," she said with a smile.

※

Hewey was down on his hands and knees, drinking from a cold mountain stream, with Biscuit a few feet downstream doing the same. "Do you smell that nasty smell?" Hewey asked, not expecting an answer from the horse.

Biscuit answered him anyway, by jerking up his head, rolling his nostrils, and backing up. Then came an awful beller from across the stream, and Biscuit backed up even farther.

Hewey scrambled to get his feet under him, the batwings on his chaps flapping. Biscuit continued his retreat.

"Slow down and we'll leave together!" Hewey said, running toward the brown horse. "Whoa, Biscuit," he said quietly, trying to calm the horse enough to catch him.

Hewey managed to grab the trailing reins and catch up briefly before the retreating horse jerked him down again and sent him rolling.

He kept hold of the reins, and when he stood again he worked his way hand over hand toward the bug-eyed brown horse. He never looked back but jabbed his left foot into the stirrup. With Biscuit still backing away, Hewey stepped into the saddle.

Finally in the saddle, Hewey was able to look across the stream at whatever was scaring Biscuit so terribly. Just then the foul-smelling beast emerged partway from the brush along the stream bank.

Hewey had never seen anything like it. The animal stood much taller than a man and bore a hump on its back as well. It was tan in color, had a long neck, and was knock-kneed. Its two-toed splayed feet were oversized. It was the most frightening and evil-looking creature he had ever seen, he quickly decided.

Biscuit continued to snort and roll his nose at the animal, which for its part only stood staring at them impassively. It chewed its cud just like a cow, Hewey noticed. He thought about shooting it, but Biscuit was on the verge of a runaway and Hewey knew he'd never be able to hit anything, even something so big.

Both Hewey and the brown horse kept wary eyes on the beast as it backed into the brush once more, spitting as it went. Hewey's eyes scanned left and right lest the animal burst out somewhere else. In time he reined Biscuit away from the creek, but he continued looking back periodically. Fortunately he never saw another hair of the wild animal.

◆◈◆

Hewey's next move was uncharacteristic for him. He was not in the habit of voluntarily seeking out law enforcement, but in this case his sense of civic responsibility won out. Up until then he wasn't even certain he had a sense of civic responsibility.

But he felt this situation was serious. If the people nearby were not aware of what was roaming the vicinity they needed to be warned. If they were aware, they should at least be encouraged to put up signs for the benefit of innocent passersby.

He was pleasantly surprised that the first town he encountered was Laramie. He had known he was on the right road but hadn't known how far away it was, exactly.

It did not take Hewey long to find the sheriff's office, and the man himself was at his desk. He seemed a holdout to the style of lawmen from the previous century, which in fact he had been.

"Tom Darnall," he said, shaking Hewey's hand before sitting down again. He gestured to a chair opposite, and Hewey sat.

"What can I do for you, Mr. Calloway?"

It did not take Hewey long to lay out his story, which produced a smile from the lawman. Hewey had not expected that. He had expected alarm or even disbelief.

"So you've seen him," the sheriff said when Hewey was done. "People around here have gone years without ever seeing him, me among them, and then there are some folks like you passing through that bump into him right off the bat."

"I didn't exactly bump into him, but I come closer than I wanted to. Does a thing like that have a name?"

"That, Mr. Calloway, is a camel," the sheriff said.

"Like them sheiks and such ride in the desert?" Hewey asked.

"Yes, I'm told the army brought some into this country before the war. It started down in Texas. They thought these camels would replace the horse, mostly as pack animals, at least, but it never worked out. I've read a good deal about it, out of curiosity since one seems to have taken up residence here." The sheriff seemed to enjoy talking about the camels.

"They say a few got loose during the project, and I heard the army sold most of them and turned some others loose. Over the years they got scattered a little bit of everywhere. I don't know how in the hell one ended up in Laramie, but it did and seems to like it."

"Well, I'll be damned," Hewey said. "A camel. I still think you need to put up signs. If that camel doesn't hurt someone, it's gonna cause somebody's horse to hurt them."

The sheriff followed Hewey outside, where the two immediately heard a commotion down the street to their right. The main street through town was narrow and made of dirt. Every so often there was a wooden water trough along the edge of the street.

In front of the more-popular establishments a few horses stood tied, and there was an occasional wagon and team as well.

The commotion was caused by a light wagon pulled by a single high-headed sorrel horse. There was no one in the wagon, and the sorrel was running full tilt down the street in the direction of the sheriff's office.

The runaway wagon passed the saloon, which had several saddled horses tied by the bridle reins to a rail along the front of the building. The horses set back as the wagon flew by, which caused the buggy horse to swerve to its right. The runaway horse missed one of the wooden troughs by about a foot, but the wagon did not. The front wheel hit the trough, which sprang a leak but didn't give ground. The wagon wheel splintered but somehow stayed on the hub. The wagon rolled on, although now with a noticeable limp on the front right. Several women screamed as the wagon flew past, and a small black dog followed as fast as it could, barking as it lost ground. The sorrel was terrified of it all.

Hewey had taken in the situation at a glance. Biscuit was tied to the hitching rail outside the sheriff's office, and he quickly pulled the reins loose and stepped on. Hewey jerked down his rope and pulled down the horn knot, tying his rope to his saddle horn. He just had time to shake out a loop before the runaway wagon came barreling past.

Hewey spurred Biscuit into a run alongside, although the horse's sense of self-preservation kept it from getting too close to the bouncing wagon. Hewey swung his loop only twice, and he had to throw a coil to make up for the distance his shying horse caused. Hewey watched with pride as the beautiful loop fell over the sorrel's head.

Given the choice, Hewey would have tried to ease the sorrel to a stop. Biscuit, however, had over the years been used to rope many hundreds of wild cattle. The best way to gain control of an unruly cow was to jerk her down and exert some authority. So just as Hewey's loop settled over the sorrel's neck, Biscuit slid to a stop on the hard surface of the street, lowering his hindquarters both to stop quickly and in preparation for the jerk he knew was coming.

Hewey, in that brief instant before the impact, remembered taking a moment to loosen his cinch before entering the sheriff's office so Biscuit could relax. He realized then that he had not pulled it tight again. Hewey had never been one to bail off a horse in a wreck, but he would have then had there been time. There was not.

The wreck was brief but violent, for Hewey at least.

The saddle was jerked forward onto Biscuit's neck, where it caught as both the front and rear cinches bunched together behind Biscuit's forelegs. Hewey was launched straight over Biscuit's head, and the first thing to hit the ground was his face. Biscuit, to his credit, never gave an inch. The sorrel horse was jerked to a stop, and the local barber nonchalantly stepped out of his shop and grabbed the reins. He looked down at Hewey on the ground and shook his head side to side. Foolish cowboys.

The sheriff helped Hewey to his feet. "Damn, Calloway. That was nice work. Maybe not the way I'd have done it, but it worked."

Hewey hurt all over, but it was his pride that took it the hardest. He felt as if the entire town was laughing at him, while in reality most of the townsfolk were only grateful. Several strangers even offered to buy him a drink, which he gladly accepted.

Hanley had told him to meet in two weeks, but Hewey had to admit that he had lost count of the days. He felt it was close to two weeks since he and Hanley had parted, but he wasn't certain if he was early or late. Hanley did not seem to be in town, but Hewey figured he would show up sooner or later.

He spent the night at the wagonyard. His aversion to spending money on hotels was only enhanced now that he had given away most of his money. Still a good trade, he figured.

CHAPTER EIGHT

Biscuit's feet were getting long, so after breakfast the next morning Hewey rode the brown horse down to the blacksmith shop, which was on the edge of town.

The blacksmith had just finished shoeing a horse when Hewey walked up. Most blacksmiths liked to begin early in the morning during the warmer months, and this one was no exception. The man was short but stout, his forearms bulging from years of hard labor. Hewey guessed his age at about sixty, maybe a little more, but the man walked as if he were twenty years older.

"Mornin'." Hewey stuck out his hand to shake. "Hewey Calloway."

"Harold Thomas." His handshake was strong and firm with nothing extra. The old man had nothing to prove. Hewey saw the palms of the man's hands were covered in calluses, and a couple of the fingers were bent at unnatural angles.

"My pony yonder needs to be shod. What do you charge?"

The man casually looked over at Biscuit. "Dollar-fifty, if he ain't a bronc."

Hewey gave a pained look, thinking of his meager bankroll. "Mister, I'm just about broke. I'm used to shoeing my own horse, but I ain't got the tools with me. Mostly I use whatever they have where I'm working. That's always got me by. What would you charge to use your tools and sell me some shoes and nails?"

The blacksmith smiled a wicked little smile. "Where you from, cowpoke?"

"Texas."

"And you say you can shoe a horse?"

"Been shoeing my own since I was a kid. Sometimes we shod the good horses at the ranches, but mostly we just rode them barefoot. But I know a little."

"Tell you what, Tex. I won't charge you a nickel, but you got to help me shoe them two mules yonder." He nodded his head outside, where two sorrel work mules stood tied to the fence. They stood half-asleep, heads hanging. Both had gray hair around their eyes, ears, and muzzles. "I just want you to pull the shoes and do the clinching. I'll do the important parts. Then I'll give you the shoes and nails for your pony there, and you'd be welcome to anything in my shop."

At cowboy wages it would take Hewey a day and a half to make the dollar-fifty the man wanted to shoe Biscuit. He figured they'd be done with all of them by noon and he could go take a nap under a shade tree.

"It's a deal, mister." He stuck out his hand.

The blacksmith shook it. He had that wicked look on his face again. "But we got to shoe them mules first."

The old blacksmith told Hewey to bring both the mules and tie them under the shade tree that was just outside the shop. He didn't want Hewey to get too hot, he said. There was a stout hitching rail that showed heavy use built under the tree, made of square timbers ten inches across. The rail was long enough for both mules with plenty of room left between them.

Thomas went to the back of the shop and rummaged around. He came back with a battered horseshoeing apron that he handed to Hewey.

"Put those on. Might save your britches." He was already wearing a shoeing apron, though one of a much newer vintage. The one Hewey buckled on showed years of use. The leather was slick and hard, and along the fronts and insides of his thighs the apron was scarred from horseshoe nails and rasps and slips of the hoof knife.

Thomas handed Hewey a pair of shoe pullers and an old hoof knife. "Start with the john mule. He's easier. Just pull the shoes and knife him out a little bit, then I'll take over. Can't have you crippling a mule for a good customer."

The old john mule stood quietly, eyes half-closed.

Hewey ran his hand down the left front leg, half expecting the mule to pick up its foot or at least shift its weight to the other side. The mule did neither. Hewey pinched the tendon running down the back of the cannon bone. The mule didn't move.

"Ol' George there, he don't help you much, does he?" Thomas was grinning.

Hewey pushed his own shoulder into the mule's shoulder, forcing it to shift its weight. He grabbed the pastern and lifted the mule's leg and put it between his own.

"This ain't my first day." He grinned at Thomas.

"We'll see, Tex."

Hewey gripped the shoe at one heel with the pullers and began rocking it toward the inside, pulling the nails loose. George, never opening an eye, cocked his right hind foot, which shifted his weight to his left front, the one Hewey was holding up. George was a big mule, a half-draft of some sort that had been bred to pull heavy loads. He was heavy. Hewey held firm and continued to work, but his thighs were burning. Sweat began to trickle from under his hat, and he could feel it running down his stomach.

He got the shoe pulled and the hoof knifed somewhat. The foot slammed to the ground when he dropped it due to the downward pressure the mule had been putting on that leg.

Hewey took off his hat and hung it on a fence post. His head was too hot for it. "Damn, he's heavy, ain't he?"

Thomas gave a look of confusion, although Hewey thought it was put on. "George, nah, he ain't bad. Keep goin', Tex. You're doin' good."

A break would have been nice, he thought, but he went to the left hind. "This mule ain't bad to kick, is he?"

"George?" Thomas was surprised. "I've been shoeing George for ten years, maybe more. He's gentle as a kitten."

Hewey appraised Thomas for a moment. Finding no sign of either humor or an outright lie, he placed his inside hand on the mule's hip and ran his outside hand down the leg, pulling forward on the back of the cannon bone. George never moved, not even an eyelid. Hewey pushed as hard as he could with his inside hand, forcing the mule to shift its weight to the other side. He was able to manually lift the leg and slide under it.

Working as fast as he could, Hewey began to pull the shoe. George slowly shifted his weight back. Hewey's legs began to tremble.

"Ain't you got one of them stands to hold up these hinds?" Hewey asked Thomas, who was now sitting on an overturned bucket, watching.

"Those are for women and children. You're doing fine," came the reply.

Hewey didn't feel fine, but he continued. When the shoe was pulled he dropped it and the pull-offs on the ground and reached for the knife. In that moment his hold on the foot slackened. The hoof slid a couple inches down Hewey's thighs, and George felt it. The big mule squatted down, stabbing his toe toward the ground. Hewey had lost what little leverage he had begun with, and George slammed his foot down on top of Hewey's.

The pain was enough that Hewey couldn't speak, much less cuss. He stood, bracing himself against the mule's hip, his heart pounding, wondering if all his toes were still attached. George was again motionless.

"Better keep that mule's toe pulled up," Thomas said, a faint look of amusement on his face. "Ol' George'll do that every time, 'less you're careful."

After a couple minutes Hewey's heart rate and breathing slowed enough for him to function. He thought about whipping the mule, and he thought about whipping the blacksmith, but he wasn't sure he could make much ground with either.

Instead he propped up one foot, then the other, removing his spurs. He rolled up his shirtsleeves and wished he had a towel to mop the sweat running down his face. He could tell his socks and even his underwear were wet with sweat.

George squatted down on the other two feet, but Hewey was better prepared. When the mule tried to stomp his hind to the ground, Hewey held the toe and kept the leverage.

"Stand up, you old son of a bitch," said Thomas helpfully from his seat on the bucket.

When Hewey was done pulling the shoes, he set his tools down and walked over to a long rectangular wooden water trough with a hand pump next to it. He was a coffee drinker by nature, but at that moment he needed water and plenty of it. He couldn't recall being this hot in some time, and he was accustomed to Texas summers.

There was a metal cup hanging from the pump by a rusty wire. The pump was primed, so water spurted out after two pumps of the handle. Hewey drank four big cupfuls, then filled the fifth and poured it over his head. He was already wet anyway.

Thomas carried a wooden shoeing box to the mule and began to work. His movements were quick and efficient, and he didn't have as much trouble with the mule.

When the left front foot was trimmed, he walked to a rack in the shop and selected a set of shoes and began shaping one on his big anvil, not bothering with the coal forge that sat nearby. He noticed Hewey watching him.

"In the wintertime when it's cold and slow I build a bunch of shoes in that old forge there. That way I don't have to mess with that damn thing when it's hot like this."

Thomas had to walk back to his anvil once and make a couple small adjustments to the shoe, closing it one lick and straightening the heels slightly.

Satisfied with the fit, he nailed the first shoe on the mule, then walked into the shop and came back out with a hind-leg stand.

Hewey's eyes got big with disbelief. He had asked Thomas

for that exact tool. "I thought you said those were for women and children!"

Thomas had an innocent look on his face. "And old men. They're okay for old men, too."

The blacksmith moved along innocently, so much so that Hewey had trouble staying mad. He might've, had he noticed Thomas grinning when his back was turned. George stood sleepily for Thomas. The hind-leg stand, rather than the man, supported his weight. Thomas made short work of the mule.

Hewey noticed that the old horseshoer, despite having so many labor-and time-induced physical ailments, was very comfortable once he was under the mule. The mule seemed more comfortable as well. It always took the man a few seconds to stand up straight afterward, though.

When Thomas was done nailing on the shoes, it was Hewey's turn again. Thomas pointed out a different foot stand, this one for finishing. Hewey was surprised. He figured the old man would make him prop the foot on his leg, just for fun. Hewey rasped the hooves down even with the shoes, then hammer clinched the nails. Noticing the change in Hewey's attitude, the mule never tried any other major tricks.

Thomas studied Hewey's work when he was done. "It'll work, I reckon. Good thing he's going to work, not some kind of mule show where people'd be lookin' at him, though." The old man walked away. Over his shoulder, he said, "Enough standin' around. Pull the shoes off that molly mule."

The molly mule was a dead ringer for the john mule, so much so that they could have been full siblings, which was often the case with working teams. Hewey was wary of her, despite her demeanor. She stood as sleepily as the john, but Hewey knew mules could be deceptive. Thomas was back, sitting on his bucket and watching. He made no observations or warnings.

"That old mule's name is Molly," Thomas said from his bucket. "Folks are real original around here."

Molly stood perfectly for Hewey, never moving, aside from swishing her tail at a couple flies and flicking her ears once when a wagon drove by near the shop. When he went for the first hind foot, Hewey looked at the hind-leg stand and then at Thomas.

"By all means," the old-timer said grandly, sweeping a hand toward the stand. "What's mine is yours."

The next three feet were as easy as the first. Thomas had no trouble with his portion, and had all four feet trimmed and nailed up in under twenty minutes. Hewey watched, trying to learn. He had shod quite a few horses but was far behind the old man in skill.

The short rest had cooled and revived him somewhat, and Hewey went to work finishing the molly mule. He moved around the mule in a counterclockwise motion that began at the front left foot, which was customary of the job. The third foot he came to was the right hind. He pulled it up on the stand and rasped the small bit of excess hoof hanging over the outside of the shoe, and then he rasped the nail ends almost flush with the hoof. He went from nail to nail, holding a large metal block under the shoe, then hammering each nail, folding it over and clinching it.

The nails on the outside gave him some trouble, because he couldn't get into a good position. His legs had begun to shake, and the foot kept trying to slip off the stand. He scooted back a few inches, trying to get some leverage. Suddenly the molly mule jerked her foot off the stand and pulled it forward and out.

Fast as a snake, she cow-kicked Hewey in the right thigh, knocking him to the ground just behind her. The mule put her foot back on the ground and stood still. Hewey lay on the ground. He didn't believe his leg was broken, but it was certainly painful.

"You better get up from there, before that bitch does it again," said Thomas from his bucket. "She'll do that now and then."

At that Hewey crawled a few feet until he felt safely out of range, then stood up and tested his leg. He wasn't sure he could beat Thomas in a foot race just then.

"You'll be all right directly, Tex," said Thomas. "Finish her up. It's about dinnertime."

The molly mule behaved like a kid's pony and never made a bobble as Hewey finished up. He often thought he could almost read a horse's mind, but not so with mules. He could never tell what they were thinking. He wasn't sure *they* even knew.

"Let's go up to the house. I bet Martha will have dinner ready."

Hewey looked down at himself. "Mr. Thomas, I'm too sweaty and dirty to go eat in your wife's house."

"Son, my wife has spent the last forty years livin' with a horseshoer. You think you're the first one she's been around that smelled like a horse?"

"No, sir, I reckon not. But let me get a drink of water first." He drank several more cups of water out of the hand pump and washed off his face, hands, and forearms as best he could.

"Let's go, Tex. We ain't goin' to a dance."

Hewey had to slow his pace to keep from outrunning Thomas on the short walk to the house, which was a small but well-kept home with a recent coat of white paint. Hewey had always been a fan of paint and thought he'd keep his own house painted, if by chance he ever owned one. There was a small flower bed along the front of the house, and beside it was a fairly large garden that showed much attention.

"Nice garden," Hewey noted.

"That's Martha's deal. She likes it, and she puts up a lot of vegetables for the winter." Thomas walked into the house, and Hewey followed, removing his hat.

The door opened into a decent-sized room with a kitchen on the right and to the left a large homemade wooden dining table. There were three places set at the table. A slim woman with gray-streaked blond hair was in the kitchen. Her face was browned and wrinkled.

"Martha, this is Hewey Calloway, come all the way from Texas to eat dinner with us. He's not much of a horseshoer, but he seems like a decent feller."

"Stop it, Harold." But she smiled, then held out her hand to Hewey. "Mr. Calloway, I'm Martha. Glad to have you."

"Ma'am, I'd like it if you just called me Hewey. And you don't have to feed me. I know you weren't expectin' company."

"Yes, I was. I saw you down at the shop and figured Harold would invite you up. He likes company, even if he doesn't act like it."

Thomas frowned at his wife but did not respond. He gestured at the table. "Sit down, Tex."

"Harold, stop that. Call him by his name." Martha was back in the kitchen. She began carrying pans and platters to the table. Thomas had not sat, and he helped his wife carry the food to the table.

"Would you like some coffee, Hewey?" she asked.

"No, ma'am. I'd prefer water."

"Better bring the pitcher, Martha. He got a little dry down there."

Following the hard work of the morning Hewey was starving, and nearly anything would have suited him. Martha set out a couple of his favorites, though—fried chicken and fried okra, plus a green vegetable he wasn't familiar with.

Martha caught his quizzical expression. "That is spinach, Hewey. I grow it in the garden. It seems to grow well in this climate."

Hewey had never met a type of food he wouldn't try and few he didn't like, so he tried a forkful.

Martha was watching him closely. "Well?"

"I like it, ma'am. Thank you."

"What do you do in Texas, Hewey?"

It took a few seconds to chew his chicken. "I'm a cowboy, work on ranches, mostly in West Texas. Spent last winter down by Durango at a line camp."

"What brings you to Laramie?" Martha was more interested in conversation than her food. Her husband was not.

"Just passin' through, headin' for Canada," Hewey said. "But I'm supposed to meet a feller here in a day or two."

"Do you have work in Canada?"

Still thirsty, Hewey took a drink of water. "No, ma'am, just sort of takin' a trip. I never seen Canada, so I figured I'd just ride up there and look it over some."

"I take it you're not a family man, then?"

"No, ma'am. Got a brother in Texas and he's got a couple boys, but I ain't seen 'em in a year or more. Probably ought to."

"Yes, you probably should." Her tone had changed some and Hewey couldn't figure why.

The conversation slowed, which allowed Hewey to finish his meal, including a couple more pieces of chicken.

"Mr. Thomas, how'd you get in the blacksmithing business?" He was genuinely curious but also felt uncomfortable with the silence.

Thomas scooted his chair back from the table. "I grew up on a little farm in Indiana and had done a little there at home. When the war broke out I joined up, knowing I was going whether I liked it or not. I told them I was good at shoeing horses and mules, thinkin' that would keep me out of the fightin'."

The old man paused, remembering. "Well, I was wrong. They made me fight all the same. I just had to shoe horses the rest of the time. Wasn't just me, though. There were a bunch of us. We couldn't keep up, there was so much work. The army had thousands and thousands of horses and work mules. That's how I learned."

Thomas had become quiet. Martha took over. "A few years after the war we came west. Laramie was growing then, and Harold set up the first blacksmith shop in town. Of course there was no actual shop building in the beginning, and we lived in a tent for the first six months. But it grew. I taught school up until a few years ago."

Hewey liked the old couple. "Do you have children?"

Both were silent, then Thomas abruptly stood and walked out the door. Martha looked at Hewey and said, "The Lord blessed us with one son, and then He saw fit to take him from us. His name was Bobby. He drowned in the Laramie River when he was nine years old. Harold was there and couldn't find him. It bothers him still."

"I'm sorry, ma'am," Hewey said. "I shouldn't have asked."

"Don't be. You didn't know. It was a long time ago. Bobby would be a little younger than you, I guess, if he were still here. I don't mind talking about him." She paused. "Harold does."

Hewey stood and carried his plate and glass to the kitchen counter. When he tried to help with the other dishes, Martha shooed him toward the door.

"You'll still be in town tonight?" she asked.

"I reckon so."

"Will you come back and eat supper with us? I'd like it."

"Yes, ma'am. I'd like to," he said.

"It's settled, then. I'll see you this evening."

"Thank you, ma'am."

Thomas wasn't outside. Hewey found him sitting outside the shop in the shade on his bucket. "I guess Martha told you about Bobby?"

Hewey nodded, not knowing what to say. After a moment Thomas nodded and said, "Bring that brown horse of yours up here. We'll see if you can get him shod."

Biscuit was good about his feet. As a colt he hadn't been, but quick retaliation by Hewey had taught him that it was easier to just stand still.

Once the first shoe was pulled and the hoof knifed out, Hewey began trimming the hoof wall. Thomas was sitting on his bucket, watching closely. While he had operated his nippers with speed and ease, Hewey was slow and awkward.

"Tex, do you have trouble with this horse gettin' lame sometimes, particularly right after you shoe him?"

Hewey glanced up but didn't take the bait. He was rasping the foot, trying to smooth out the mess he'd made with the nippers. Thomas went to his anvil and began shaping a shoe, which he brought to Hewey. It fit perfectly. Hewey knew it would have taken him several trips to the anvil to get it right.

He began nailing on the shoe. His first nail came out about right, but the second was far too low. Hewey pulled it and began driving another. He hit it awkwardly with the little hammer and the nail bent sideways.

"Those nails are expensive. Try not to waste all of 'em." Thomas was back on his bucket.

The comments didn't help, but Hewey got the first foot nailed up. Thomas came and inspected it. "You do know those nails are supposed to be in a straight line, don't you?"

Getting used to the jokes, Hewey smiled. Thomas kicked his bucket along the ground to get a good viewpoint of the hind foot Hewey had begun to work on. Thomas was frowning at the result.

"Are you a good cowboy, Tex?" asked the old man.

"Pretty good, I reckon."

"It's a good thing, because you're a damn poor horseshoer. Get out of there and let me do it. This is too nice a horse for me to sit and watch you cripple him."

Hewey paused and thought that over, pride causing him to consider refusing. Good sense took over, and he stood and allowed Thomas to help him.

When they were done with Biscuit, they each sat on buckets in the shade cooling off. Hewey smoked a cigarette and Thomas occasionally spit a stream of tobacco juice. He asked Hewey where he was staying.

"At the wagonyard yonder." He nodded toward the nearby building and pens. "Me and Biscuit both."

"Tell you what, Tex. Turn that brown loose here in one of my traps," he said, pointing behind his shop at several small grass pastures. "There are a couple stalls in the barn you can sleep in, or you can pitch your bedroll under one of these trees if you'd rather. Save you a little money."

"Thank you," Hewey replied. "You don't know anybody needin' some work done for a couple days, do you? I'm runnin' a little short on spendin' money."

Thomas gave it some thought. "Tell you what. I've got five

young horses in one of those traps, never been handled much but they're not too bad. I'll give you a half dollar a saddlin' to put the first few rides on them. Then maybe one of these town kids can take over."

That was far better than cowboy wages in Texas, which was Hewey's measuring stick. He accepted.

"I'll pen them tonight if I catch them up for water, or you can take ol' Brownie and lope around them in the mornin'. I got some good corrals in back you can use."

Late in the afternoon Hewey moved his camp and set up under an old oak tree behind the barn. The weather was clear and pretty, the nights pleasantly cool. Better for sleeping outside than in a dusty horse stall. He joined the Thomases for supper and retired early, tired from the day's labor.

CHAPTER NINE

Hewey had breakfast with the Thomas family then saddled Biscuit and rode into one of the small pastures behind the shop and gathered the broncs, which Thomas had told him were all long three-year-olds he had traded for the year before. They were nice, big-boned colts with large feet and hairy legs. Northern horses.

Thomas had carried his bucket from the shop and was again sitting in the shade watching. "Last summer we staked them out a few times when we branded and gelded them. They're sorta gentle but they ain't been handled much. I used to do better, but it gets harder ever year."

There were two stout wooden corrals built side by side with a gate between them. One had a worn snubbing post in the center. It was a good setup, Hewey thought, except that horses had been walking on it so long the ground was packed hard as rock.

"Hell, I ain't hittin' the ground anyways," he said to Biscuit.

Rather than work on foot, Hewey decided to rope the colts off Biscuit. He thought they might be just gentle enough not to fight too much. He sorted a bay colt into the next corral, then shut the gate between them. The colt stood staring at its companions across the fence, and Hewey effortlessly dropped a houlihan over its neck.

Startled, the colt ran left along the fence. Hewey took a wrap around his saddle horn. Biscuit had the inside track in the corral, so Hewey kept the rope tight around the colt's neck but moved with it, slowing it without jerking it or completely choking it.

It took two laps around the pen for the colt to give, but soon it accepted the idea that the rope was master.

Smart colt, thought Hewey.

Thomas had produced an old but stout breaking hackamore since Hewey did not have one. It took a few minutes and several brief fits by the bay colt, but he was finally able to ease Biscuit alongside and slide the hackamore on the colt. He led the colt around the pen a couple times, then to the snubbing post, where he tied it.

Done with Biscuit for the moment, Hewey tied him outside the pen. He unsaddled the brown and carried the saddle into the corral. This would have been easier with some help, he mused, but then again there were only five broncs.

He petted on the colt a couple minutes, then sacked it out briefly with the saddle blanket. He was able to saddle it without tying up a front leg, although it did jump out from under his saddle once.

He led the colt in a couple circles so it could feel the cinches, then took a short hold on the left hackamore rein and pulled the bay's head around toward him. As soon as the colt gave its head, Hewey grabbed the saddle horn and stepped on. He held the colt's head to the side for a few seconds, then gave it slack.

Uncertain, the bay stood still. Hewey mashed lightly with his legs, and the colt remained still. He tickled it with his spur rowels and got nothing. Finally, Hewey took his right hackamore rein and lightly swatted the colt on the hip. Frightened, the bay leaped forward, landed hard, and leaped again. Then it stopped and stood. Hewey swatted it again, and the colt moved off at a trot. Eyes wide, it kept turning its head to look back at Hewey, but it moved forward.

Every couple laps or so Hewey would pull its head around to one side or the other, forcing the colt to change direction. Twice he sawed on the reins until the colt stopped. After only a few minutes, Hewey eased the colt to a stop and stepped off quickly, wary of a kick that didn't come.

"This one will make a horse," he said to Thomas.

The old man had been watching attentively. "I believe he just might."

The next two colts went about like the first, although a big gray colt crow-hopped a few licks. Thomas left and returned with a water jug he offered Hewey.

Tired of saddling and unsaddling Biscuit, Hewey decided on the fourth colt to rope it on foot. There were two broncs left, a brown colt with a short tail and a pretty sorrel that was the best looking of the bunch but also seemed to be the wildest. Hewey threw a loop for the sorrel, wanting to be done with him. The colt saw it coming and stepped to the side, and the rope flew past and caught the brown instead.

"Nice loop, if that'd been the one you were aiming at," came a taunt from outside the corral. Hewey ignored it.

The brown colt would not lead out of the pen and Hewey didn't have Biscuit to drag it, so he or more or less drove the colt into the next corral and the snubbing post. From there the colt was fairly easy to work with, and Hewey was able to get a short ride on him without much trouble.

The sorrel colt was left alone in the corral, and he rolled his nose and snorted at Hewey as he entered the corral, rope in hand. Hewey eased within range and waited until the sorrel looked across at the other colts, then he quickly brought up his rope and threw a houlihan. The colt somehow saw it coming and turned its head to the side, and the rope fell in the dirt.

This ain't his first time, thought Hewey.

"Two misses and it's my turn," called Thomas from his bucket.

"You can try him right now if you think you can do better."

"No, you go on there, Tex," Thomas said. "Be a shame for an old man to embarrass you."

Hewey built a new loop. The sorrel was watching him constantly now, unconcerned with the other horses. Hewey brought up his arm and turned the rope over in a fluid motion. The sorrel anticipated the throw and sidestepped to its left, but Hewey had never turned loose of his rope.

Never slowing his arm, he continued the arc in a backhanded swing, releasing a second after the colt first dodged.

The loop dropped over the colt's head, and Hewey pulled the slack out of it. The sorrel immediately ran to the right, and Hewey squatted down and braced on the end of the rope. But instead of dragging Hewey, when the sorrel felt the pull on the rope it instantly turned and faced him.

Hewey gave it a few seconds, then gently pulled on the rope. The sorrel walked two steps toward him. Hewey pulled again. This time the colt came three steps.

"This ain't his first day," Hewey said. "You sure this sucker ain't been handled?"

"I bought them as raw broncs, but who knows? You can't trust anybody anymore. Bunch of lying sumbitches everywhere these days."

Playing out slack as he went, Hewey walked to the fence and took down the hackamore he had hung there. The sorrel was standing still, so he thought he might slip the hackamore on it without the use of the snubbing post.

Moving slowly and coiling his rope as he went, Hewey eased toward the sorrel, which rolled its nose even more but didn't move. Hewey walked toward its shoulder, and the colt let him. When he touched the sorrel on the neck the skin quivered, but still the colt stood firm. Hewey gripped the hackamore hanger with his right hand and the bosal with his left. The colt never moved as he slipped on the hackamore. Just as he finished tying the throat latch the sorrel struck with its left front foot, pawing Hewey down the back of his right leg.

The blow didn't knock him down, but it almost did. The sorrel leaped backward several feet and stared, wide-eyed.

Hewey looked down the back of his leg at the rake mark left by the hoof. He looked back at the sorrel. "You silly son of a bitch," he said. He still held one hackamore rein, and he gave it a light tug. The sorrel stepped toward him.

Hewey turned and walked, and the sorrel followed. "Uh-oh," said Thomas from his bucket.

"Yes, sir. I believe this'un might be somethin' besides a raw bronc," Hewey said, leading the sorrel toward his saddle.

"Look in his mouth, see how old he is," suggested Thomas.

"*You* come look in his mouth," Hewey replied. "I done been pawed once today."

He held the sorrel rather than snubbing him as he placed first a Navajo blanket then his saddle on the bronc's back. The sorrel quivered at their touch but did not move. Hewey stood next to the front leg as he cinched up the saddle, wary of both the front and hind feet. He was watching the sorrel, and it was watching him out of the corner of its eye. Neither trusted the other.

The sorrel was humped up so much the rear of the saddle was raised several inches. Hewey forced the colt to untrack, then led it in a couple small circles. He looked down thoughtfully at the hard ground, cheeked the bronc, and stepped on.

For two seconds the sorrel stood quivering, then it sucked in air and leaped straight up. When its feet hit the ground it bawled, and instead of moving forward as Hewey expected it jumped to the left and reached up and cow-kicked Hewey's right spur, nearly pulling it from his boot. The hackamore reins were long and heavy with leather poppers on the ends. Hewey reached back and whipped the sorrel under the belly on the side the kick had come from.

"Stay with him, Tex," hollered Thomas from outside the corral. He was no longer on his bucket but standing excitedly.

The sorrel bucked honestly for several jumps, but when that didn't loosen Hewey it gave up and began running around the corral, slamming Hewey's outside leg into the fence. The tactic would have worked better had the corral been round, but at every corner Hewey had a couple seconds of relief. In the first corner he swatted the sorrel with the hackamore rein, which did not deter the bronc. At the next corner Hewey reached his toe out as far as he could, then slammed his spur into the sorrel's side.

The sorrel grunted as the air went out of it, and it leaped

toward the center of the corral and stopped, sides heaving. Also out of breath, Hewey sat still for a few seconds before pulling the sorrel's head to the left and swatting it with the other rein. Sweat running down its neck and flanks, the bronc followed his simple cues. Hewey rode it at a walk, then a trot, and after just a couple minutes he pulled it to a stop and stepped off.

As soon as Hewey hit the ground, the sorrel reached up and swatted at him with its hind foot, but Hewey was ready and easily dodged it. He instantly kicked the bronc in the belly between the two cinches.

Thomas laughed. "Mean little bastard, ain't he?"

Hewey stood, breathing hard from the exertion. "Damned sure won't do for women and children."

The sorrel didn't give much trouble as Hewey unsaddled him. All the colts were turned back into the trap for the night. Hewey set his saddle on Biscuit's back without cinching it up, so Biscuit could carry it to the barn for him.

When Hewey had things put away, Thomas motioned for him to sit down in the shade near him. "Sit down a minute, Hewey." It was the first time Thomas had called him by the correct name.

Thomas handed him a half-full whiskey bottle that had been hidden in his shop. Hewey took a small pull and handed it back.

"You were pretty good out there, with them horses," said the old blacksmith.

"Thank you. It's about the only thing I've ever been good at, that and punchin' cows."

Thomas tilted the bottle back, taking a healthy swig. "You never thought about settlin' down, gettin' a place of your own or even a steady sort of job?"

Hewey was quiet for a few seconds. Everyone was always mashing on him about this, advising him on what he ought to be doing. He never told them what they should do with their lives. "Reckon I just never felt the call," he said finally.

"I like you, Hewey, so I'm going to tell you something and then be quiet about it. You're damned good with those horses, about as good as I ever seen, but you ain't a youngster anymore.

I can tell that by lookin' at you. Time'll come when you'll look around and there won't be nobody there and you'll wish you had a wife and some kids. Life's a lot more fun with kids. Believe me. I know it both ways."

Hewey didn't know what to say, or if he was really supposed to say anything. He rolled a cigarette, and the two men sat in silence.

Finally Thomas stood up and looked down at him. "Time catches up with all of us. Even you, Hewey Calloway."

CHAPTER TEN

With half the afternoon to kill and knowing he had some pay coming for topping off the broncs, Hewey decided he might buy the new shirt and socks he had been meaning to purchase for the last several weeks. He considered catching Biscuit but decided against it. The brown horse was tired from hard use all morning, and Hewey had noticed a mercantile just down the street. Against his nature he set off walking.

There was one horse tied outside the mercantile building, and Hewey was surprised when he recognized it as the nice gray gelding that belonged to Bob Wilson. Although he had invited Wilson to meet them in Laramie, Hewey had never really thought he would see Wilson again.

Wilson was nowhere to be seen outside, so Hewey went on into the store. Wilson stood at a shelf about halfway back in the store, and when he heard the door open he turned quickly, alarm in his eyes. He relaxed when he saw it was only Hewey.

Pointing a finger at Wilson like a gun, Hewey said, "Pinkerton Detective Agency. You're under arrest." Then he burst out laughing.

Wilson barely smiled, then looked at the storekeeper with concern. The man was listening but did not seem to think much of it. He had seen his share of foolish cowboys over the years.

The two men shook hands, but Wilson said, "That's not

funny, Hewey. Everywhere I look I see a Pinkerton detective or a sheriff or somebody else out to get me."

Hewey grinned at him. "Shoot, Bob, I'm sorry. I didn't mean no harm."

"I thought about what you said, about how your Ranger friend might could help in some way." Wilson was fidgeting, obviously nervous. "I just don't know what else to do. Is he around somewhere?"

"He's supposed to meet me here, but I ain't seen him yet. He'll show up directly."

Wilson had a few meager food supplies in his hands, and Hewey asked where he was staying.

"I've been camping outside of town for several days. I been riding into town, hopin' to run into you somewhere but ain't. I been too nervous to spend much time in any town lately."

"I'm staying behind the blacksmith shop right down the road here on the edge of town. Come with me and you can camp there. I've got room under my tree, long as you don't snore too much."

Wilson paid for his few supplies, and Hewey realized he was again forgetting to buy some new clothes. Maybe tomorrow, he thought. They found Thomas shoeing a riding horse outside his shop. The owner was nowhere to be seen, probably gone into town.

Thomas dropped the foot he was working on when they walked up. "This here's a friend of mine from Colorado," Hewey said. Wilson stepped forward and offered his hand.

"Harold Thomas," said the blacksmith, shaking.

"Bob Wilson."

Thomas held the much younger man's hand for too long. Wilson had no idea why, and neither did Hewey, at least not at first.

"I'm sorry. I had a son named Bob," Thomas said finally. "He'd be about your age now, maybe a little older."

Wilson didn't know what to say, other than "Yes, sir."

Hewey broke the spell. "Reckon it'd suit you for Wilson to camp back there with me? He's a little short on spending money and shy of crowds."

Thomas was still shaken. He always got that way when hearing his son's name, but this one hit harder because of the age similarity. "That's fine, Hewey. Just put his horse in there with yours." He walked off without another word.

❖

The next morning Hewey and Wilson were up before the sun, as was their usual. They had a small fire going in the makeshift fire pit Hewey had made a couple days earlier out of several large rocks and some scrap metal he found outside Thomas's blacksmith shop. The metal was suspended across the rocks to hold his pans and coffeepot.

Martha Thomas had extended a perpetual invitation to her table, but Hewey didn't want to overdo it. This morning he was frying some bacon that they would eat with some biscuits left over from the day before. He wanted to get an early start on the broncs, and Wilson had offered to help.

After breakfast and with the sun just rising, Wilson saddled his gray and loped around the broncs grazing in the horse pasture. Hewey noticed that Wilson had loped around the horses but slowed and brought them into the pens at a trot. "That boy knows what he's doing," he said to Biscuit, who was eating a small can of oats Hewey had put out for him.

Wilson drove the broncs into the water lot and allowed them a few minutes to drink, since they probably would have come in for water early in the morning on their own. Once they had drank their fill, he pushed them into one of the corrals Hewey had used the day before. Still horseback, Wilson shook out a loop.

"Catch that pretty little sorrel first, if you can," Hewey said from outside the corral.

Wilson waited for a chance at the sorrel, and he even stirred the horses some, hoping to force an opportunity, but the little horse was too wise. He stayed behind the other horses, against the fence with his head down.

Hewey soon ran out of patience. "Oh hell, catch any of them if that little jackass keeps it up."

Wilson ignored him and forced the broncs to move. His rope had so much speed on it that it sang as he brought it up. Hewey could hear the rope buzz as Wilson pulled the slack, tightening the loop around the neck of the pretty sorrel bronc. The colt took a couple steps but didn't run. Wilson nudged his gray horse nearer, taking up the slack. He reached down and petted the sorrel a few seconds, then turned and asked it to follow. The sorrel remembered the previous day's lesson, and felt some security following the gray horse, so it led behind.

Hewey helped Wilson through the gate with the bronc, and then he handed the younger man a hackamore. He noticed two men walk up outside the corral, but he couldn't see them well because the sun was low and just behind them. Moving slow and talking quietly, Wilson slipped the hackamore on the sorrel. That done, he loosened the rope around its neck and slid it off, handing it down to Hewey.

Still talking to the sorrel, Wilson dallied the hackamore rein to his horn and turned his gray perpendicular to the bronc, giving Hewey room to work. Hewey didn't have a brush with him, so he ran his hands around and under the sorrel where the saddle would fit, making certain there was not a sticker or burr stuck somewhere. He'd probably have enough trouble without a sticker causing even more. Either out of patience or more likely resignation, the sorrel stood mostly still while Hewey saddled it.

When the sorrel was saddled, Wilson asked what Hewey wanted him to do.

"Wait 'til I get on, then hand me that rein. Then just ride off and I bet he'll foller you. Ought to make this all go some easier."

The sorrel's eyes grew wide when Hewey stepped on, but it followed Wilson's gray horse when it walked off. Three steps later, Hewey felt the sorrel tighten underneath him.

"Here we go," he said quietly to Wilson.

The sorrel bunched his hind end underneath him then exploded forward, running across the corral and almost into the stout wood fence. Although Hewey thought the sorrel was about to crash into the fence, there was nothing much he could do. He pulled the left hackamore rein as hard as he could, but that had no discernible effect. Just before it hit the fence the sorrel sucked back under itself and reversed directions, coming up bucking.

Hewey had not expected the move. He rode through it, but he was loose for the first couple jumps. He grabbed the saddle horn, something he absolutely hated to do. But what he hated worse was hitting the ground. The jarring he took was worse after he grabbed the horn, but Hewey got his seat back. The sorrel began bellering, which didn't make a bucking horse any harder to ride but always made for a good show if there was anyone watching.

In control again, Hewey turned loose of the horn and began spanking the sorrel on the hip with every jump. The bronc quickly gave up the bucking and began loping around the corral. Wilson loped alongside then slightly in front, and when he eased to a trot the sorrel followed suit.

Hewey had Wilson change direction several times and finally stop, and he cued the sorrel to do the same each time. Soon Wilson rode to the center of the corral and stopped, and Hewey had enough control that he was able to make some simple maneuvers on his own. After a few minutes he felt the bronc had learned enough for the day, and he stepped off.

Hewey took a couple minutes to pet on the bronc, which eyed him but did not offer to strike or run. Then with Wilson following he led the sorrel over to the fence. He knew one of the spectators was Thomas, and when he drew nearer he saw the other man was Tom Darnall, the sheriff he had met when he first came to town.

Thomas was grinning at Hewey. "Tom just told me about you roping the runaway buggy horse the other day and saving the town from certain disaster." The blacksmith began to laugh at his own wit. "If only you'd had some kind of help, like a banker, or maybe even a barber."

Both the older men broke into serious laughter at that. Hewey tried to act pained but couldn't help it. He began laughing at himself so hard he broke into a fit of coughing. He had known

Thomas would hear the story eventually and harass him about it. It had been inevitable.

When they got control of themselves, Thomas pointed to Wilson, who had been standing quietly, not knowing the joke. "Tom, that there is Bob Wilson. He's a friend of ol' Tex the horse roper here, though don't let that fool you. He seems like a decent feller so far."

Wilson stepped forward and stuck his hand through the fence so they could shake hands.

"Don't let Hewey lead you astray 'round here," Thomas jokingly advised Wilson. "Ol' Tom here is a hard case, and he has a badge to back him up. He's the Albany County sheriff."

Wilson froze for an instant. He felt like Darnall was appraising him harder than necessary. Hewey was the only one to notice Wilson's discomfort. It was too perfect an opportunity to pass up. "Well, he's fallin' down on the job. He's got a fugitive in his midst and hasn't done anything about it."

Wilson shot a worried glance at Hewey, and the older men stared at Hewey as he paused for effect.

"That camel is still out there somewhere and is a danger to public safety. Almost got me killed."

Sheriff Darnall shook his head, smiling at Wilson. "It was bad enough I had to listen to this sort of nonsense from Harold every time my horse needed to be shod. Now there are two smart alecks around here I got to tend with," he said.

"Speaking of," said Thomas. "I better get your old horse shod 'fore there's a stickup or some such and you need him."

The two headed for the blacksmith shop, but Darnall turned back to Hewey and Wilson. "That was fun to watch you two with that sorrel bronc," he said. "Hell of a job, both of you, and I know a little about that sort of thing."

The other four broncs were relatively easy to saddle and ride, particularly compared to the sorrel. The men were done soon after noontime, and they rode into town to eat at the café. Wilson was hesitant to go into public but gave in at Hewey's insistence. When they returned to Thomas's shop they found him set to begin shoeing a team of light pulling horses, a big job for anyone, regardless of age.

"Care for some help, Mr. Thomas?" asked Wilson.

Thomas looked at the two of them. "Can you shoe a horse better than your pal there?"

Wilson looked down at Biscuit's feet. "Can't say for sure, sir. His work here looks pretty good to me. Looks like good shoe shaping and nice nails. Clinches are a little rough."

Hewey grinned at Thomas.

"Sure, Bob," said the old blacksmith. "I could use the help."

"You need my help?" asked Hewey.

Thomas shook his head. "No, thank you. I believe we'd be better off if you went and bought a new shirt or something. Take your time, Tex."

Bob Wilson and Hewey Calloway were up early again the next morning, stirring over their fire, making coffee and a meager breakfast. Wilson had told Hewey the evening before that Thomas had asked him to help shoe several horses that were coming to the shop, so Hewey would be alone with the broncs. It would be their third ride, and it was past time for them to graduate to some outside riding.

He would have preferred using the broncs on a drive or some other type of actual ranch work, but that just wasn't the situation. He figured he would make a big circle outside of town on each horse. The broncs were ready to see something new and come back tired, and Hewey wanted Thomas to get his money's worth.

He began with the short-tailed brown, which was showing some potential. Hewey was able to saddle the brown without much trouble. The bronc had a hump in its back initially, but it never acted on it. Its eyes got wide when they passed the blacksmith shop, which had a line of horses and mules tied to the fence outside. Both Wilson and Thomas were working under the shade tree, although the morning was still cool. Hewey could feel the sun's warmth and knew it would heat up soon enough, though. Two men Hewey did not know stood watching the work, laughing and talking to one another.

Hewey took the dirt road headed out of town. The brown spooked at several wagons and horses and once a small boy who was playing in the yard of his house. Several times Hewey had to pull the bronc's head around to the side when the excitement became too much and it wanted to run. Soon Hewey left the road and trotted down to the Laramie River, following it for a couple miles until he hit a fence and had to return to the road.

"Damn fences everywhere anymore," he said to the brown colt.

He turned back toward town. Hewey was proud of the brown and had been talking to it, telling the horse how well it had done. They were almost to Thomas's shop when a teenaged boy riding a bicycle turned a corner ahead of them and came their direction.

Hewey had seen a handful of bicycles and personally thought they were silly. The brown bronc had evidently never seen a bicycle and thought it was terrifying. It stuck its head up in the air, high enough Hewey could have touched the top of its head without leaning forward. The reins went slack, and he had no control whatsoever.

The bicycle came on, the teenaged driver oblivious. "Easy now." Hewey was talking quietly and calmly. The brown was not comforted. "Don't do nothing we'll both regret."

The brown began moving its front feet, wanting to go somewhere but not sure where. The bicycle came on, the rider now smiling in a friendly manner. He wore a little cap on his head, and when he tipped it to Hewey and said good morning, the brown couldn't take it anymore. It wanted to run but could not take its eyes off the monster, so it began running backward down the short road that led to Thomas's shop. Hewey tried to pull its head to the side, but the brown didn't listen and Hewey had no leverage because the bronc's head was almost in his lap. He spurred it once, but that did nothing but speed up things.

Hewey was certain he had never gone so fast backward. They passed by the horses and mules tied to the fence, but the brown didn't notice. He was still snorting at the bicycle, which had stopped so the rider could watch the show.

Behind him, Hewey heard Wilson yell at him to watch his head. He looked back to see they were headed straight for Thomas's shade tree, with two horses still tied underneath. The lower branches were high enough not to bother a man on foot, but they were too low for a man horseback. Hewey ducked forward, and he had to lean to the side because the brown's head was still so high it was in the way. Hewey knew it wouldn't, but he hoped the horse would bang its fool head on a branch.

Thomas went one way and Wilson the other, and the brown colt and Hewey went in between. The two horses tied under the tree wanted to move but were tied to the stout hitching post. The brown crashed into the first, knocking it sideways into the other. Unfazed, the brown never slowed. It ran over Thomas's wooden shoeing box, scattering tools. Horseshoe nails went everywhere.

"What in the hell are you doing, Tex?" shouted Thomas.

The first they had seen was the brown running backward toward them. They knew nothing of the bicycle.

The brown kept going, but the two horses tied beneath the tree were both setting back on their lead ropes. Thomas watched as one of them got on top of his wooden shoeing box, scattering tools and stomping it into several pieces.

"Get off my box, you stupid son of a bitch!"

The brown continued until it backed into a corner made by a fence on one side and the blacksmith shop on the other. It stood rocked back on its hind legs, trembling.

The horse and Hewey both watched the boy on the bicycle pedal away, no longer interested.

The two men Hewey had seen earlier stood smiling, wanting to laugh but feeling it might be unwise considering Thomas's current state of mind. Wilson wisely kept quiet also. Thomas stood glaring at his demolished shoeing box and the tools scattered everywhere.

The brown finally untracked, and Hewey nudged it toward the tree.

Thomas looked up at him, his eyes aglow. He spoke quietly. "You have all this country." He gestured around with his arm. "Why in the hell are you running a horse backward through my work area?"

Hewey looked sheepish. "Hell, it wasn't my fault. That kid on that derned bicycle scared my horse." He pointed toward the road.

Thomas, Wilson, and the two men all looked toward the road, which was empty, not a bicycle to be seen. Thomas turned back and glared at Hewey, then stomped into his shop to get his spare shoeing box and a magnet to pick up all his nails.

Wilson looked at Hewey and began giggling, which set Hewey to laughing, which in turn set off the two men who had been watching.

Just then Thomas came stalking out, a battered and repaired old shoeing box in his hand. "What in the hell is so funny!" Thomas growled. He was smiling, though.

CHAPTER ELEVEN

Hewey Calloway's brown horse was easy enough to spot in the dim electric lighting that filtered out of the saloon windows, and Hanley Baker reined in beside him.

Hewey himself was just as easy for Baker to see once he made it indoors. He was busy shuffling cards and entertaining the other patrons with tall tales.

"What took you so long?" Hewey asked from the table where he sat sipping a beer.

"Looks like you were expecting me," Baker said when he reached Hewey's table.

"I've been expectin' you for days."

"I was busy tending to family matters," Baker answered. "You don't understand families, do you?"

"Sure I do," Hewey answered. "Got one of my own."

"And you see yours even less than I see mine," Baker said. "But at least I think about mine, and pay 'em a visit every now and then. How long has it been since you've seen Walter and Eve and the boys?"

"Awhile," Hewey said.

"I'd make it a year or more," Baker ventured, "and I know you're not much for writing."

"Dern it, you just walk in and start griping at me?" Seemed like everywhere he turned there was always someone trying to tell him how to live his life.

Baker could tell he had struck a chord and chose to leave it alone. Best he could tell with his time with Hewey Calloway was that there wasn't much going to change him anyway.

Baker had one drink, then stood, ready to go. "Well, now that we've found each other, I'm goin' to turn in," Baker said. "It's gettin' late."

"I'll go with you, since you broke my hot streak with the cards. I was just about to get rich when you come in."

"I bet," Baker said.

The two mounted their horses, and Hewey led the way through the darkness toward the blacksmith shop.

"Where you been stayin'?" asked Baker.

Hewey told him about the blacksmith shop, and that he figured Baker would be welcome to stay as well.

"Harold Thomas, the blacksmith up here, he had some broncs he needed broke, and I needed the money, so I been riding 'em for him. He's lettin' me camp in the back."

"I thought you had a big stash left over from the winter. What happened to that?"

"I give it away, most of it anyway."

"You're going to die a poor man someday, Hewey."

"I don't plan on dyin' for a long time. Don't know if I'll be poor, but I'll be happy when I go, I guarantee you that."

Baker did not know anyone else would be at Hewey's camp, so he was surprised when Wilson stood as they rode up.

"Hanley Baker, meet Bob Wilson," Hewey said with his crooked grin.

"You knew him years ago as Bobby. And I believe you met Hanley here a long time ago. His uncle was your neighbor back in Colorado."

Hewey's grin got bigger as he watched Baker and Wilson connect the dots. "You'll have plenty to talk about in the morning."

"I'm not waiting 'til morning," Baker said. "Bobby, Hewey told me about your troubles and it's all I've been able to think about. Hewey believes you, and I think I believe you. I'm going to unsaddle my horse and mule, and after that I want you to tell me everything so I can sort it out in my head."

Hewey laid on his bedroll smoking a cigarette and listening to Wilson tell his story, which was punctuated with many questions from Baker. Hewey had heard it before, and he finally crawled into his bed and drifted off to sleep to the sound of their voices.

Early the next morning Hewey saddled the pretty sorrel colt, planning to take it on a big enough circle that it came back tired. The sorrel had made progress, but Hewey still had to watch it closely or it would paw him when he was on the ground or buck when he was on its back.

Wilson was committed to helping Thomas again, which had become a regular event. Thomas appreciated the help, but Hewey could tell the old blacksmith enjoyed the company as well. Over breakfast Baker said he would stay close. He was still mulling over the bank robbery, trying to make sense of it.

Hewey took the road southwest out of town. The Laramie River followed the same general path, meandering along the southeast side of the road. The sorrel had a hump in its back but resisted several temptations to act on it. Hewey held the sorrel to a trot for several miles, and it finally let down and relaxed somewhat so Hewey slowed to a walk for a while, enjoying the scenery. Traffic was light on the road; all morning he had seen only two men on horseback and one wagon carrying a man, woman, and several kids. The sorrel spooked at the noisy children but held itself together.

Soon enough Hewey grew tired of the road, and he found a trail that closely hugged the riverbank. It was prettier along the river, and Hewey had nowhere in particular to be, so he followed it. Late in the morning he turned a small bend and was momentarily taken aback by the scene only a stone's throw in front of him. The trail ahead fell several feet down to the river on one side, and on the other side of the trail was a rise of about six feet. The trail itself was only a few feet wide.

A pretty young woman sat on a trembling black tobiano paint horse at the edge of the trail. Both the young lady and her paint horse were staring at a small mountain lion that was crouched under a sagebrush on the bank above them, not much more than head high to the lady. The young mountain lion seemed as surprised at the situation as they were, but it held firm, hissing at the lady and her frightened mount.

Taking in the scene, Hewey doubted the lady or her horse were in much danger from the mountain lion itself, but the paint horse was so frightened it appeared that it might do something foolish like fall off the drop-off into the river below.

Hewey was only twenty-five yards or so away, but the sorrel colt had also seen the young mountain lion and had shut down. Neither the lady's horse nor his own cared for the smell or sight of the lion. Hewey had run across several mountain lions over the years but had never been this close to a live one. He reflected briefly that horses might be severely frightened of all mountain lions, even skinny half-grown ones such as this.

The sorrel seemed all too willing to leave the scene, but the lady's paint still stood locked in place. Hewey attempted to frighten the cat by yelling. The noise drew its attention, but its hissing only grew louder. The young lady looked at Hewey desperately, but her horse never took its eyes off the cat. The sorrel colt was fidgeting and wanting to turn, but Hewey kept it more or less in place. He thought about dismounting and throwing rocks to scare away the small cat, but he knew without a doubt that if he stepped off he would never be able to hold the sorrel bronc and would be walking back to town.

"Take a deep seat, ma'am," Hewey hollered, "it's about to get noisy!"

He drew his carbine and took a shaky aim as the sorrel continued to fidget. He had to hold the hackamore reins loosely so that he could also hold the carbine, which gave him even less control. He was concerned the sorrel's fidgeting might cause him to shoot the woman or her horse rather than the lion, so he had to wait until the sorrel grew still.

Long ago Hewey had heard somewhere that it was easy to shoot a gun off a horse—one time. The next shot might not be so easy. He felt that might be about to prove true here. He squeezed off a shot and missed, but the loud report of the rifle and the whine of the ricochet so near caused the little cat to wheel and run, bounding down the riverbank until it disappeared around a bend.

Hewey saw only the first of that scene because he was dealing with a mild runaway from the sorrel. He had some trouble gathering up his reins while holding the carbine, but finally he was able to pull the sorrel's head around and get it stopped. He kicked it over toward the lady's horse, which still stood frozen on the edge of the drop-off. Moving in slowly, Hewey quietly picked up the woman's left bridle rein, then slowly walked away from the edge.

The paint horse followed, calming gradually.

"Easy now," Hewey spoke to the horse; the sorrel had already quieted down, which helped to calm the woman's mount. The woman was still breathing deeply but soon relaxed enough to thank Hewey profusely.

"You saved my life," she said to Hewey.

"Aw, I don't know about that," Hewey replied. "It was kinda' tense there for a minute, but you did a lot of it yourself, keepin' control of your horse."

"I would like to know who I'm thanking," the woman finally said. "I'm Daisy Baker."

"Baker?" Hewey asked in genuine surprise. "Any relation to Hanley Baker?"

Now it was the young lady's turn for surprise. "He's my uncle. And you?"

"My name's Hewey Calloway. Nice to meet you, ma'am."

"I was hoping to meet you, Mr. Calloway. I just never imagined it would be under these circumstances."

"You take what you can get, I reckon," Hewey said with his

crooked grin. "And the name's just Hewey. What in the world were you doin' out here?"

"I was hoping to find Uncle Hanley," said Daisy Baker. "I knew he went to Laramie to meet you. I have a newspaper story that may help explain something that has been bothering him for the last couple weeks. He was so preoccupied with that bank robbery he told me about, and then the day after he left I saw this story. I thought about attempting to mail it to him, or trying to reach him by telegram or even telephone, but I wasn't certain how to find him."

"I don't put much stock in newspapers," Hewey said, "but if you think it's all that important, I'll be happy to take it to him. He's back in Laramie. Or you could ride along with me if you'd rather."

"I believe I will head back for now. This has been enough excitement to last me for some time. I'm not an adventurer, Mr. Calloway, just a schoolteacher out of her place."

"If you'll call me plain old Hewey, I'll be glad to help you."

The goal of the day had been to tire out the sorrel bronc. By the time they made it back to town Hewey felt he might have accomplished that but had tired himself even more. He found Wilson and Baker in their campsite and told them about unexpectedly running into Baker's niece. Baker was as surprised as Hewey had been and initially seemed angry at Hewey for the mountain lion scare. There were a few sharp words before Hewey got out the entire story and convinced Baker he had not somehow led Daisy into trouble.

"I'm sorry, Hewey," Baker finally said. "She's the closest thing I have to a daughter, and I'm too protective sometimes."

"Apology accepted, you grouchy old jackass."

Baker looked at Hewey a moment then laughed, defusing the situation.

"Your niece thought you'd be interested in this newspaper story. I never took the time to read it. Don't have Ol' Sorrel broke enough to read a newspaper off his back yet."

Hewey helped himself to a plate from the pots Baker and

Wilson had left at the edge of the fire to keep warm. They had both eaten but saved some for him.

"You know," Hewey said after his first mouthful. "I may name that sorrel bronc Hanley, since he's so damn hard to get along with sometimes."

Wilson laughed at that, but Baker ignored him. "What's that paper say about the robbery?" asked Wilson.

Baker scanned the front page, then turned to the next.

He read silently for a moment.

"It's an editorial," he said finally.

Neither Hewey nor Wilson responded. Baker got the feeling they didn't know what "editorial" meant.

"Just read it to us, Hanley," said Hewey. "It'll save all sorts of time."

WHAT HAPPENED TO OUR BANK?
By Stanley Lessiter, editor

Almost six weeks have gone by since the bank robbery here in our normally tranquil town of Green Ridge, and Community Bank has yet to reopen its doors. Lack of a banking institution is troublesome to be certain, but even more concerning is the absence of Mr. Charles Booker, bank owner and relative newcomer to these climes. Mr. Booker was originally applauded for his resolve when he joined the posse seeking the alleged bank robber.

However, whispers could be heard among the posse members when they returned with neither the bank's money nor the banker himself. It is not this paper's intention to lay blame against Mr. Booker for any possible wrongdoing, but both sound minds and account holders deserve a better explanation of that day's events and Mr. Booker's subsequent behavior.

Wilson sat quiet. Hewey had finished his meal and sat rolling a cigarette, thinking. Finally he asked, "Why was that so important your niece brought it all this way?"

Hanley smiled, knowing he had been on the right track and feeling some excitement at the prospect of following it even further. Even old coon dogs still like to follow a trail. "It means that some of the people in Green Ridge are doubting the honesty of their banker, just like I was. It means Bobby here might not hang after all."

"That'd probably be for the best," Hewey allowed.

Baker looked at Wilson. "You said you heard two men after the robbery, right?"

Wilson nodded. "Best I could tell, Mr. Baker. I only heard two voices, then I only saw two men. I think only one of them saw my face. But it all happened so fast, and I was in a big hurry to get out of there, what with being shot at and all."

"Tell me exactly how it happened," Hanley said. "Go slow, try to remember everything."

Wilson sat quiet for a moment, obviously thinking. "I was riding toward the bank, heading south down the street. The bank wasn't open yet, but it was almost opening time. I wasn't quite to the bank when I heard two voices from beside the bank. There's a gap there, between the bank and the barbershop next to it."

Hanley was leaning forward, listening intently. "What were these men saying that caused you to stop, or to pay attention?"

"I guess it was more how they were saying it than what they said, at least at the beginning. They just seemed so, so . . ." Wilson paused, searching for the word. "Intense, I guess would be the word. They were trying to be quiet, but their words were harsh. One was telling the other that he needed to tie down the saddlebags filled to bursting so they wouldn't fall off, and then the second said they still had to kick in the door. I never understood that, why they had to kick in the door *after* they had been in the bank. That's it. That's all they said."

"How did they figure out you were there?"

"I was dumb, Mr. Baker. I should have turned and got out of there, but I peeked my head around that building to see who they were. The fat one saw me and started fumbling for his gun.

I got out of there as fast as my gray horse could run. They shot at me several times but never hit me."

"Did you get any shots off yourself?"

"Mr. Baker, I don't even own a gun aside from my old rifle, and there was no time to draw that one, even if I'd wanted to. It was duck and run."

Hewey had been quietly listening, but he asked, "Why didn't you go to the sheriff, or whatever law they have there?"

Baker gave Hewey an appreciative look. Hewey had a good point.

"I would have, believe me, but they were shooting at me and one of them was hollering about a bank robbery. I'd have never made it out of that town, I guarantee you."

"You're probably right," Baker agreed. "These fellers aren't dumb. That much is obvious. If you heard those voices again, could you recognize them?"

"I think so, but I'm not making any promises. They both had an accent you don't hear much in this area."

"What do you mean? What sort of accent?"

"I don't know. Some kind of Yankee accent. I don't know how to describe it better."

"Well, Bobby, that's a start," Baker said.

"I've got some snooping to do," Baker said, "and I'm hopin' the local law will help me out. This newspaper editorial is short, but it gives me some ideas. That's where the snooping comes in."

"Will it help that you were a Ranger, Mr. Baker? When it comes to getting help from other lawmen, I mean."

"Sometimes it helps and sometimes it makes it harder. Depends on what they think of the Rangers."

Baker reached into a pocket and pulled out something, then pitched it to Wilson. It was once a silver Mexican coin, but Baker had long ago paid a silversmith to saw out several pieces, leaving a star in the center. Rangers were not issued badges, but most had their own made or even crafted one themselves.

"If we were in Texas, that would mean plenty," Baker said. "Up here, I don't know. We're a little rough around the edges occasionally, especially some of the earlier Rangers. That reputation has gotten out ahead of us sometimes. I've always tried to play it pretty straight, but not everybody does. I find it best to kinda pitch my hat in the door before I give too much away.

"Either way, I'm going to ride over to Green Ridge and look around, maybe ask a few questions," Baker went on. "There's a lot you can learn close up."

Baker gave Hewey a stern look, the one he used when he was about to give orders or gripe at him. "Hewey, you and Bobby need to stick together; one bunch of two will be easier for me to find than two bunches of one. It'd be better if you could stay right here, together, 'til I get back. Can you do that?"

"Dammit, Baker, stop talking to us like we're little kids or somethin'. I still got these broncs to ride, and Mr. Thomas is about ready to hire Bobby full-time or maybe even adopt him, so we're fine. We'll be right here."

"I'm sorry, Hewey. Sometimes I get a little tight in situations like this. Ask my old Ranger company, they'll tell you the same thing."

"I know it." Hewey grinned at him. "Just don't be such an old hard-ass."

Baker ignored that and went on. "Whatever y'all do, look out for Murphy and avoid him. He may be a Pinkerton man, but I don't trust him. Something still doesn't add up with him."

CHAPTER TWELVE

Baker left before the sun was up, heading generally southwest. He rode hard, keeping to a steady trot. It was a pace he could sustain fairly easily, twenty or thirty years earlier. The first night he was tired, the second he was exhausted and sore, and when he rode into the small town of Green Ridge before noon on the third day he was hurting. He rode past the bank, which sat dark and quiet, the front doors closed. The city marshal's office was easy to find.

There was a man with a badge pinned to his shirt sitting in a rocking chair on the wooden porch. He had been watching Baker as he made his way through town.

Baker gingerly stepped down from his bay horse. His entire body ached, but it was his knees that hurt him the most.

"Name's Hanley Baker," he said, extending his hand to the man on the porch.

"Ray Martin," the marshal replied with hesitation, but he shook Baker's hand. "I can't put my finger on it, but I get the feeling there's a badge in your gear somewhere. When you've worn one long enough, you get a sense of it."

"I know what you mean," Baker answered. "It's a Ranger badge."

"I don't have any use for Rangers," Martin said flatly, and started to turn away. "I've heard things about the Rangers that give me pause."

"Have you ever worked with one?" Baker asked.

"No," Martin replied, "and I'd just as soon keep it that way."

"I've worked with some local law that didn't measure up, either," Baker said. "But sometimes that's the only way to get the job done. Newspaper here acts like your banker might have robbed his own bank. I'd like to know a little more about that."

Martin had been turning to walk away but stopped. "I'd like to know a *lot* more about it," the marshal said. "Why would a banker rob his own bank?"

"Because that's where the money is," Baker replied. "A small bank doesn't cost much to set up—a used safe, mostly. The real money's what's inside the safe."

"A banker robbing himself? I've never heard of such a thing," Martin scoffed.

"It's pretty rare, but it happens. I've heard of it before," Baker said. "Besides, he's not robbing himself, he's robbing his customers."

"And what brings a Texas lawman all the way up here to look into it?"

"I'm retired and it's personal business, nothing official," Baker answered.

"Then I don't owe you anything," Martin said, turning his back again and starting toward his office.

"Looks like that rocking chair gives you a good view of what happens in your town."

"It does," said the marshal. "I've caught a little hell about sitting down on the job, but I can see most of the town from right there."

"Were you there when the bank was robbed?"

"Matter of fact, I wasn't even in town. I was testifying at a trial in Denver."

"Did people around here know you'd be gone then?" Baker asked.

"Yes, sir, several did." The sheriff sat down in his rocking chair, his attitude no longer so combative. "Hell, the way people gossip around here I guess everyone probably knew."

"Did the banker, Mr. Booker, ordinarily use the side door or the front door of the bank?"

"The front door. He always used the front door," said Martin. "He liked to make a big show of opening and closing the front doors of the bank."

"I suppose you've noticed that broken window glass yonder," Baker said with a level voice as he gestured with his chin at a building about fifty feet away. "The one with the fresh bullet hole nearby."

Martin paused and Baker knew he had him.

"Passed by it when I came into town," Baker continued. "Figured you'd seen it by now."

Martin did his best not to admit that he was in the dark, but it was all over his face.

"Anyway," Baker continued, "if there's no further business between us, I won't take up any more of your time." He stepped toward his bay horse.

"I can't imagine a couple of bullet holes could tell a man much," Martin said, clearly trying to save face.

"Probably not," Baker conceded. "Just strikes me as funny that there are bullet holes over yonder, lined up like they came from alongside of the bank, not near the front door."

"You seem to have an idea why that might be," Martin said.

"As I hear it," Baker went on, "the man who was shot at and didn't shoot back had nothin' to do with the bank robbery, just found himself in the wrong place at the wrong time. At least that's how I hear it."

The marshal stood up quickly. "You know this feller they been huntin'?"

"Yes, sir, I do."

"And you believe him?" Martin asked.

"I'm sure inclined to," Baker said.

"Why?" Martin asked.

"Because his story adds up," Baker answered. "And because I've known him since he was a boy. I knew his folks even longer. People don't change their stripes all that much. I reckon you've seen that over the years."

"You drew me right into this thing, didn't you?" Martin asked. "A man could resent being manipulated."

"Yeah, some men could, but I'm hoping you're a better man than that."

The marshal didn't care for that. "Does this innocent man of yours have a name?"

"Bob Wilson," Baker replied.

Martin paused and then broke into laughter.

"You can't be serious," he said between chuckles. "I've heard of better aliases dreamed up between the bar and the saloon doors."

"His folks probably weren't trying to create an alias," Baker said, "just raise a little boy."

"Well, sir, that little boy has a bounty on his head now. The bank depositors pooled what little they had left and had me send it out on the wire. It ain't much, only a hundred dollars, but people will be lookin'."

Baker grimaced at that news. "Well, I hope to figure this out before some fool shoots him. I wish you'd keep your eyes and ears open here."

"I'll do what I can," Martin said. "Just don't ask me to stretch the truth."

"Wouldn't do it for you and wouldn't ask you to do it for me," Baker avowed.

"You should know this. I've gotten several telegrams from sheriffs in Colorado and Wyoming saying a Pinkerton agent named Murphy was there, huntin' for our bank robber."

That set off alarm bells for Baker, particularly that Murphy had been in Wyoming also. "How about this Murphy? How'd he get involved in this deal? That is a private agency. Pinkertons shouldn't even be involved unless someone hired them."

The marshal scratched his graying beard. "That I can't tell you, but it's somethin' I've wondered about myself, many times.

The fellers who joined the posse told me later he was here that morning and just took over. Told them he was a Pinkerton passin' through. They didn't question him."

"So you've never met Murphy?"

"No, sir, they were long gone by the time I got back from Denver, and I didn't know how to find them. The posse came back, but Booker and Murphy never have."

"This may be an odd-sounding question," Baker said, "but does your banker Booker have an unfamiliar accent?"

"Come to think of it, he does," Martin replied. "Talks like some sort of northerner."

"So does Murphy," said Baker. "I ran into him in Silverton not too long ago. Your witness, Bob Wilson, never saw the robbers but heard them. They both had unusual accents, for this country.

"Those Pinkertons came out of the northeast," Baker went on. "Good men, from what I've heard, but there are always bad apples."

"So Murphy's for real?" Martin asked.

"Hell if I know. He could be," Baker answered, "but maybe more important is that they probably know each other and may have for some time. I'm going to do some more snooping, see if I can figure this out. I'd take it as favor if you'd do the same around here. I'm thinkin' these fellers may be trying to get an innocent kid hung for their crime."

Baker thought for a moment, absentmindedly rubbing a sore hip. "How long has Booker run the bank?"

"Just about a year. Couple of prospectors found a little color just north of here a few years ago, then maybe two years ago some more claims began paying off. Good bit of money started coming to town, and not long after that Booker showed up and opened the bank. That doesn't make him guilty of anything in my mind, though. We *needed* a bank."

The sheriff watched as Baker carefully stepped onto his bay horse, the stiffness and soreness showing. "Anything else you need from me?" asked the sheriff.

"Just that I'm hoping that when the need arises, you'll tell what you know," Baker answered.

Martin nodded his head willingly. "I'll tell all I know, but that's damned little at this point."

※

Hanley Baker had not been gone from the camp behind the blacksmith shop for half an hour before the plan to stay put began to fall apart. Wilson sat reading the local newspaper, which Thomas had given him when he was done with it the day before.

"Anything interesting in yesterday's newspaper?" Hewey asked Wilson. "It's a lot easier to let you read it than read it myself."

Wilson laughed at Hewey's honesty before flipping the paper open and scanning the headlines. "Here's something that might interest you," he said after a bit of scanning. "The Cheyenne Frontier Days are goin' on."

The news rarely held much interest for Hewey, but this certainly did. "Cheyenne? That's one of the big ones."

"So they claim," Wilson agreed. "I've never been."

Hewey was quiet for a moment, as deep in study as he ever got. "Let's go," he said finally.

"Are you serious?" Wilson asked. "Mr. Baker really wants us to lie low."

"That thing's gonna' be crawlin' with people," Hewey pointed out. "Nobody will notice us."

"I have an itchy feeling about it," Wilson cautioned.

"Nobody will know we're there unless you plan to win the whole thing," Hewey laughed, "and even I couldn't do that."

"I wish I'd overlooked that headline," Wilson said.

"Too late now," Hewey insisted. "How long does it last?"

Wilson studied the paper, moving his lips as he read. "It says here it's on Saturday, Monday, and Tuesday."

"What day is this?" Hewey asked.

"This is Sunday. We missed the first day."

"Damn, it'll take us nearly two days to get there. Get your

stuff together. If we leave now we'll be there in time for the last day."

Wilson stared at the ground in front of his feet for half a minute. "I sure don't think this is a good idea. I guarantee you Mr. Baker won't like it."

"Oh hell, what could go wrong? Besides, Baker ain't necessarily in charge around here."

"No, I guess he's not," Wilson sighed. "But it might be better if he was."

CHAPTER THIRTEEN

The closer Hewey and Wilson got to Cheyenne the more people they began to encounter, most headed toward town but a few headed out. With the exception of some families, those leaving town all appeared tired and perhaps hungover. A few sported bruises. Hewey idly wondered if those marks came from the rodeo or the celebration.

Brimming with excitement, Hewey grinned at Wilson, who did not seem to share his enthusiasm. "Hot damn, this must be some kind of rodeo! I'm glad you come up with this idea!"

"Oh yeah, me, too," Wilson said dejectedly. He wasn't glad at all.

The street was full of horses, teams, and people as they rode into town. There were a handful of automobiles scattered throughout the crowd, causing problems. A white banner hanging over the street caused a good many of the horses to shy as it gently flopped in the breeze.

The banner read WELCOME TO CHEYENNE FRONTIER DAYS.

They rode past the train station, where dozens of people were disembarking from a short train that was made up of nothing but passenger cars. Hewey whistled at the excitement.

"Where do you reckon all them people come from, and are they here just for the rodeo?"

"You got me," Wilson said dejectedly. "This is my first time, too." The growing crowd was making his stomach turn sour.

It was not difficult to find the rodeo grounds. They just followed the flow of the crowd through town. It took some time to find a spot to tie their horses, because every available piece of fence or hitching rail was already overloaded with tied horses.

It took another half an hour to find the small wooden building that held the office where the contestants entered the day's events.

"Come on," Hewey said. "Let's go enter the bronc ridin'."

"Nope. Not me. This is your deal. I ain't no bronc rider. I'm not entering."

Hewey grabbed Wilson by the upper arm and pulled. "Oh, come on. It'll be fun. When you get old you'll look back on this day and be glad you done it."

"I'm afraid if I keep hangin' around you I'll never make it to old age," Wilson said, but he followed Hewey inside.

※

Contestants were allowed down in the arena, so Hewey and Wilson elbowed their way through the crowd carrying their saddles. They finally found a gate and walked along the fence in front of the grandstands. Both were uncomfortable in the large crowd. Neither had ever spent much time around so many people, and it was worse for Wilson since he half expected to see Murphy staring at him through the sea of people.

Wilson gave Hewey a worried look. "I'm not liking this too much. I feel like Murphy is about to stick a gun in my ribs."

"Hell, I heard that announcer say there's six thousand people here today. That don't even include the people who was *already* in this town. There ain't no way he'd ever spot us, if he was even here."

"What do you mean 'us'? It's me he's after. Not you."

"Now don't be ungrateful," Hewey chided ridiculously. Then he pointed toward the end of the racetrack. "Now looky here."

They had missed the stake race, but just then seven Indians were lining up at a starting line far down the track. The announcer nearest them shouted through his megaphone that the Indian Pony Race was about to begin. First place, he shouted, would pay fifteen dollars.

"Well damn, I should have entered on ol' Biscuit," Hewey complained.

"I don't believe you qualify," Wilson said. The official rules of the race did actually state "for Indians only," although Wilson was only guessing since he had never seen them. He had never seen the rules for any rodeo event, ever.

Just then the starter fired a pistol in the air. Four of the horses immediately left the line at a run, two balked at the shot but were quickly encouraged into a run, and the last horse ran backward in fright until it was swallowed by the crowd. It never emerged.

The Indian jockeys all dressed like cowboys but rode their ponies bareback. Two even had war bridles on their horses. Two horses quickly established dominance and maintained the lead through the half-mile race, battling only each other for the lead. Hewey noticed the crowd cheering for one horse or the other and realized he had missed a betting opportunity.

Oh well, Hewey thought, *knowing my luck I'd have probably bet on that sucker that ran backward at the startin' line.*

The two lead horses passed in front of them, the Indian jockeys leaning forward almost on their horse's necks. One rode a sorrel paint, the other a bay. Both horses looked as if this was not their first time to run a race. The bay crossed the line half a length ahead, and the crowd erupted into a mixture of groans and cheers, depending on how they had wagered.

"Them boys can ride," Hewey observed.

"LADIES AND GENTLEMEN," the announcer shouted through his megaphone. "DON'T GO FAR. UP NEXT WE HAVE A SPECIAL TREAT FOR YOUR VIEWING PLEASURE. DIRECT FROM THE BOOMING METROPOLIS OF DESERT SPRINGS, NEVADA, WE HAVE MISS BER-

THA SIMMONS, BRONC RIDER EXTRAORDINAIRE, WHO WILL DEMONSTRATE TO ALL THESE MEN WHO LABEL THEMSELVES BRONC STOMPERS THE *PROPER WAY TO RIDE A BUCKING HORSE*."

Down the track a couple hundred feet from Hewey a middle-aged man riding a big sorrel horse led out an even bigger bay horse, this one carrying a saddle but no rider. Following behind was a slim young lady wearing tight brown riding britches and an even tighter blue shirt that showed off her considerable assets. She had long blond hair in two braids and wore a flat-topped hat.

"LADIES AND GENTLEMEN," boomed the announcer. "MEET MISS BERTHA SIMMONS. BEHIND HER THERE IS THE FAMED BUCKING HORSE BRIMSTONE, KNOWN FOR THROWING ALMOST EVERY RIDER FOOLISH ENOUGH TO FORK HIS BACK."

Hewey's eyes were locked on Bertha Simmons. Without looking he reached out and poked Wilson in the side. "I think I'm in love. I heard about this. They call it love at first sight."

Wilson rolled his eyes. "I'm sure she'll feel the same way," he said. "If she ever sees you."

Bertha Simmons waved at the crowd, then walked up to the big bay horse. She said something to the man holding its head, then grabbed the saddle horn with both hands and put her left foot in the stirrup. She had to bounce a couple times on her right foot, which delighted Hewey.

Bertha swung into the saddle and sat still aside from a slight adjustment to the hackamore reins. The big bay horse stood motionless.

Bertha said something else to the man on the snubbing horse, and he turned her loose. Instantly the big bay horse jumped straight up with its entire body save its head, which went down. At the height of the jump Bertha reached back and quirted the bay horse across the hip. The horse squealed midair, then came down and began bucking hard but rhythmically. Bertha alternated between quirting and spurring, having no difficulty staying in perfect time.

The bay horse bucked along in front of the grandstands, and the crowd cheered wildly. Hewey watched wide-eyed. Wilson watched, although with more objectivity. "She knows that horse," he said. "This isn't her first time on him. Probably takes him around and puts on shows like this."

Hewey didn't take his eyes off Bertha. "Dammit, watch your language."

Wilson furrowed his brows and considered responding, then decided it just wasn't worth the effort.

The bay horse had bucked past them and to about the center of the grandstands, when the man on the big sorrel horse loped alongside and reached down and grabbed the hackamore rein. Bertha grabbed the man around the waist and jumped behind him onto the sorrel. The bay immediately quit bucking.

Wilson raised his eyebrows in appreciation. "Well, that was slick, I admit."

"Damn right." Hewey still couldn't take his eyes from Bertha. "I gotta go meet her."

"Right now? We better stick around close. We go off chasin' women and we're liable to miss the buckin' contest."

"Hell, yes, right now," Hewey said as he began walking toward Bertha, still carrying his saddle. "You see an angel like that you don't wait around."

Wilson wondered how Hewey survived day to day. He had never met anyone so free to follow any whim or idea that struck him. With a sigh he picked up his own saddle and followed. The announcer was readying the crowd for the roping contest, while in front of the stands another special event was being held, this one where a cowboy attempted to ride a wild steer without the aid of either rope or saddle. Hewey did not even look. He was locked on to Bertha Simmons, whom he could see over the crowd, still on the back of the big sorrel horse.

A boisterous crowd had gathered around Bertha, slowing Hewey's progress. For a couple minutes it looked as if he might still make it to her, but then the man riding the big sorrel turned and headed away through the crowd, still leading the bay bucking horse and with Bertha still behind his saddle.

Hewey moaned in anguish, then began pushing harder through the sea of people. Wilson followed as best he could.

They both heard the announcer shout through his megaphone, calling all contestants in the bucking and pitching contest to the front of the grandstands to draw horses.

"Oh, hell," muttered Hewey. He looked at the retreating Bertha Simmons, then looked toward the center of the grandstands. Wilson saw that he was deciding if he could catch Bertha and still get back.

"Don't try it. We came all this way for the buckin' contest. You can find her afterward."

Hewey thought about it, knowing Wilson was right yet not wanting to admit it. Then he began grinning.

"I tell you what I'm gonna do. I'll win this buckin' contest, and I bet she comes and finds *me* afterward."

"Yes, I'm sure she will," said Wilson, who was not at all sure. Hewey had a look of reckless determination that gave Wilson an unsettling feeling.

"Well, let's go then," Hewey said as he headed the other direction. "We sure don't want to miss the draw."

A paunchy middle-aged man stood in the center of a small crowd of younger cowboys, counting them, as Hewey and Wilson walked up.

The man frowned at them. "You in the bronc ridin'?"

"Yes, sir," answered Wilson.

"You're late," the man said. "Don't nobody be late when it's your turn to ride."

Hewey stiffened, and Wilson whispered to him. "Easy, now."

"My name is Jess Nolan," the paunchy man said. "I own most of these broncs and am in charge of this event. We'll lead in the horses a couple at a time, and you boys saddle them yourselves. If one needs eared down or somethin', get your partner to help you. We ain't doin' it for you."

"Personable son of a bitch, ain't he?" Hewey whispered to Wilson.

Nolan paused and glared at Hewey. He had not heard the words but could guess the gist. "You boys ride 'til you get bucked off or the horse quits. There are two judges, but I ain't tellin' you who they are. Don't need no bad sports takin' it out on our judges again."

Nolan took several slips of paper from his shirt pocket, removed his hat, and placed the papers inside.

"Everybody take one. That will be your horse. I don't want to hear any bitchin' about it later."

The bronc riders filed by, each reaching in the hat for their draw. There were a couple smiles and a couple groans when the names of known horses were found.

Hewey was last to draw. His slip said STEAMBOAT. A bell rang in the back of his mind, but he couldn't place it.

"Say, anybody here heard of this horse?" he asked loudly. "Name's Steamboat."

A wicked grin came across Nolan's face. "Hell, boy. They all heard of Steamboat. You're either a long way from home or some kind of punkin' roller not to have heard of him."

Hewey bowed up at that. "Listen here, mister. I ain't no damn punkin' roller. You'll see that directly."

Wilson stepped between the men. Hewey was becoming more and more riled, and Nolan seemed to be enjoying it.

One of the other bronc riders had been watching with interest. He was young and rail-thin. "You really never heard of Steamboat, mister?"

Hewey cut his eyes to the young bronc rider but softened when he realized the boy was being genuine.

"No, I haven't. What's the big deal?"

The kid was shy but began talking quietly. "He come off the Two Bars up north of here. Some say he's the best buckin' horse there ever was. He's been in some Wild West shows, and they bring him to the big contests like this. He's been ridden, but not many times. You get him ridden, mister, and you're sure to win."

Hewey was nodding his head and grinning, then he slapped his leg. "Well, hell, this is just right!" he exclaimed.

The teenaged bronc rider was confused but went on. "They say he broke a bone in his nose when they gelded him. I don't know if that's true, but he makes a funny sound when he bucks. That's why they call him Steamboat. He sounds like a steamboat on a river."

Still grinning, Hewey looked at Wilson. "Bob, I tell you what. If this horse is as tough as they say, Bertha will be watchin', and she'll see me ride him. I couldn't have planned it any better."

There was no set order for the eight bronc riders to compete; they rode in whatever order their drawn horses were caught and brought into the arena. Two men on big, strong snubbing horses brought in the first two bucking horses.

Hewey was impressed with the looks of these horses.

They were big-boned, big-footed, hairy-legged northern horses. He tingled with excitement and confidence, and he couldn't wait for his turn.

The teenaged boy who had told them about Steamboat had one of the first horses brought into the arena. It was a big roan with feet as big as dishpans.

"You got somebody to help you, son?" asked Hewey.

"No, sir, I don't."

"Well, come on. We'll help you."

The boy carried his saddle to the roan, which stood at the end of the short rope held by the man on the snubbing horse. Hewey eased up to the roan, ran his hand down its neck, and grabbed an ear. He'd seen many muggers bite horses' ears, but he never cared for it. He had always walked away with a mouthful of horse hair.

Wilson helped the boy saddle the roan, and Hewey tightened up as the teenager climbed aboard.

"LADIES AND GENTLEMEN," boomed the announcer through his megaphone. "IT APPEARS THAT FIRST UP

IN THE BUCKING AND PITCHING CONTEST IS A LOCAL COWBOY, YOUNG ELTON MURRAY, RIDING SUN DEVIL."

When Murray was ready the snubber turned the bronc loose and Hewey released its ear. The roan reared straight up and teetered at the brink of going over, then crashed to the ground and left bucking. Hewey had seen ranker horses, but he had not seen many better bronc rides. Young Murray spurred the roan every jump and never seemed uncomfortable.

Hewey let out a yell of encouragement for the boy, as did many in the crowd. The roan bucked a large circle, then finally stopped and stood, sucking air. Murray stepped off and away quickly, wary of a strike that never came. The man on the big snubbing horse eased up and caught the hackamore reins. Hewey and Wilson rushed over and helped Murray unsaddle the roan.

Hewey slapped Murray on the back. "Now that was a bronc ride! You sure had his number."

Murray grinned at the praise. "Thank you, sir."

They paused to watch the next rider, who made it two jumps before being thrown over the bronc's head. The next pair of cowboys both made good rides, although Hewey felt like Murray likely still held the lead.

Just then the snubbing horses returned, one leading a plain-looking sorrel with three white socks and a head big enough for two horses.

"LADIES AND GENTLEMEN, PLEASE WELCOME TO THE CHEYENNE FRONTIER DAYS FAMED BUCKING HORSE STEAMBOAT. AND ALL THE WAY FROM UPTON COUNTY, TEXAS, WE HAVE HUGH CALLOWAY."

Elton Murray offered to help, and he got on Steamboat's head while Wilson helped Hewey with his saddle. The horse stood still, almost relaxed. Before Hewey tightened his cinches, he reached under and unbuckled the leather keeper between the front cinch and the flank cinch.

"What are you doing, Hewey?" asked Wilson.

Hewey pushed his flank cinch back and pulled it tight.

He'd seen several cowboys bucked off over the years when their cinch keeper broke and the flank cinch moved back. It never failed to make a horse buck hard.

The man on the snubbing horse had been watching, also. "Son, that ain't necessary. This pony will be hard enough to get by without it."

"Hell, I didn't come all this way for second place." Hewey winked at Murray, who was looking back at him. "It'll take something big to get by that young peeler up there on this pony's ear."

Hewey stepped in the saddle, and Steamboat never moved. He settled into the saddle, mashed his heels down, and pointed his toes out. He had the hackamore reins crossed over Steamboat's neck, and he held the reins in both hands about a foot apart. When he was ready, he nodded his head and said, "Turn him loose!"

Murray let go of the ear and jumped back, and the snubber turned Steamboat loose. The sorrel stood still for a moment, and Hewey felt him take in a deep breath. He tucked his chin, knowing something was coming.

Steamboat exploded forward, taking several running steps. The flank cinch grabbed him far back, and he ducked his big head and began bucking. The first jump jarred Hewey's teeth. The big-headed sorrel was serious. Steamboat began making his trademark sound, a sound similar to a straining steamboat engine pushing its load up a fast-moving river. The unusual sound might have unnerved Hewey had he the time to think about it, which he didn't just then.

Hewey rode through the second and third jumps, but Steamboat's kicks kept getting higher and the landings harder. Feeling confident, Hewey reached forward with both feet and raked his spurs along Steamboat's shoulders. The horse hit the ground, changed leads, and spun to the right suddenly. Hewey hadn't expected the move and felt his body slide left, loose in the saddle.

Steamboat had been born with a natural ability to buck, and

most of those who knew the horse felt he enjoyed it. But *all* of them agreed that the horse was as good as any bucking horse going at feeling a weakness and seizing it.

Steamboat felt one such weakness when Hewey got loose and his weight shifted left. The steamboat sound grew more intense, and the horse leaped in the air and sunfished, his body nearly parallel to the ground, his left side six feet off the hard surface of the arena. Steamboat's body seemed to hang in the air, then he kicked his feet and righted himself on the way back down.

When Steamboat hit the ground Hewey was without his right stirrup. He still had both hands on the hackamore reins, fighting for his balance. There had been a moment when he might have recovered if he had grabbed the saddle horn, but sure-enough bronc riders disdained to claw leather, particularly in public. That moment had passed anyway, and both Hewey and Steamboat knew it.

Steamboat jumped forward, landing hard on his front feet and kicking up with his hinds. There was talk later from knowing spectators that they had never seen him kick so high. Hewey might have ridden through it, had he begun the move with a good seat and both stirrups. As it was he was shot over the front of the saddle, clearing Steamboat's big head by several feet.

The ground had been packed hard by the hooves of the horses and the boots of so many cowboys, and it did not give as Hewey's body slapped into it. All the air left his body with an audible sound, and it took several excruciating seconds for his lungs to reinflate. Wilson and Murray helped him to his feet.

Murray was grinning ear to ear. "That was some bronc ride, mister! I never seen a horse buck like that!"

Breathing was becoming a little easier, and Hewey was beginning to feel better. "I reckon that ol' bronc knew he had to bring his best to unseat me."

"Well, I'd say it worked," Wilson said stoically.

Hewey did not see the rider who was up just after him since he was still recovering, but Wilson told him the cowboy only made it a few jumps before he was thrown.

Wilson was up in the final pair of horses brought in, and he had drawn a tall, lanky gray gelding with big feet, a small hip, and a very long back. Hewey figured some sort of scrub stud horse must have broken into the pen with someone's work mare, resulting in an animal so unusual.

Murray once again had an ear, and Hewey was helping Wilson get the saddle on the gray. The other bronc rider had his horse saddled first. He didn't make it two jumps before he hit the ground.

Hewey grinned and poked Wilson in the ribs. "All you gotta do is get him rode and you'll be in the money."

"That might not be that easy," Wilson said. "Nearly everyone has been bucked off so far."

"Just do the opposite of what I did. What could go wrong?"

Wilson heard his name shouted from the megaphone and was soon mounted. He took a deep seat, ducked his chin, and hung on. The heavy-footed horse pounded the arena floor, but Wilson took a death grip with his thighs and ankles, locking his spurs in the cinch. It wasn't pretty, as Hewey's ride might have been had things ended differently, yet all the big bronc's spinning and stomping failed to dislodge Wilson.

"Hang in there," Hewey yelled over and over, or at least that's what Wilson thought he heard.

The big gray bucked in a large counterclockwise circle, and Wilson stayed with him every jump. Finally the gray bucked into the fence and quit. Wilson jumped off and clear of the horse.

The crowd cheered for him, although not as loudly as they had for Hewey, who didn't even get his horse ridden.

The bronc riders had to wait only a couple minutes, then the announcer with the megaphone called out the winners. No one was surprised to hear that Elton Murray had come out on top, except perhaps Murray himself. The boy was grinning so much Hewey was afraid he might hurt himself.

Wilson placed third, which set Hewey to grinning as much as Murray had been.

"Hot damn!" Hewey practically yelled at the more reserved Wilson while slapping him on the back. "Drinks are on you!"

They stayed for the rest of rodeo, and afterward Wilson went to the office and collected his prize money. He was surprised to find it was thirty-five dollars.

"That's more'n a month's cowboy wages," Wilson said.

The pair found their horses and put their saddles back on them. They drifted along with the crowd toward the saloons in town. Murray came along, although he seemed hesitant. Hewey asked what he had won.

"Fifty dollars, a new saddle, and some new boots," Murray answered. He seemed in a daze over it all.

"Well, I'm travelin' with a couple regular high rollers." Hewey grinned.

Most of the contestants headed for the same place, and Hewey and Wilson figured that was the place to be. Hewey had planned to force Wilson to buy the drinks with his winnings, but half the patrons of the crowded bar wanted to buy drinks for them, some because Murray had won but most because Hewey had put on such a show. They all wanted to pat him on the back, and many told him how it would have been the greatest bronc ride of all time, if he had only gotten Steamboat ridden.

One intoxicated young cowboy told Hewey that he felt certain he was dead, as hard as he slapped the ground.

"I wondered that myself, for a minute there," Hewey acknowledged.

After an hour and far too many free drinks, Hewey had hit the point of no return. Wilson was far more sober, since there were no free drinks for third place, and he was trying unsuccessfully to steer Hewey toward the door.

"Let's go find us something to eat, and then someplace to camp, away from this crowd," Wilson pleaded.

Hewey put his arm around Wilson's shoulder and stared at

him for an uncomfortably long time. "We will, Bob Wilson. In a little while."

"We best go tend to our horses. They're still tied outside."

That gave Hewey pause, though briefly. "Them horses will be standing up wherever they are. Don't matter if they're in a fancy stall or tied to that rail out there. Don't matter to them."

Just then a small crowd came through the door, and several cowboys near the door let out yells. Hewey looked up in time to see the flat hat and long blond braids that he knew belonged to Bertha Simmons.

"Now we're getting somewhere!" he exclaimed, already in motion toward the figure of Bertha Simmons, who had turned and headed toward the corner of the barroom, where it was slightly less crowded.

Against his better judgement, Wilson followed behind.

He hated to leave Hewey alone in this shape, but he was considering it.

Hewey had no plan what to say to Bertha, which was probably just as well. He had at times in the past planned out what to say to women, and he could not remember a single time it had worked out well.

Bertha stopped and was speaking to several men. Her back was still to Hewey. As he drew near her he settled on beginning the conversation with "pardon me, ma'am," but that was as far as he got. Fortunately, before he could speak one of the men with Bertha recognized him. "I'd like to buy a drink for you, mister. This is the feller that put on the show on Steamboat earlier!"

Hewey could not have planned a more perfect introduction. Bertha slowly turned toward him, and when she completed the turn the air left him almost as severely as it had when Steamboat threw him to the ground.

Bertha was not at all what Hewey had expected. She wasn't nearly as pretty as he had pictured, not even close. She smiled at him, showing a large wad of chewing tobacco between her cheek and gum. She turned slightly and spit a stream of brown juice on the floor, and a little bit dribbled down her chin. Bertha either did not notice or just didn't care.

She stuck out her hand. Hewey shook it, though timidly.

"I seen that ride on Steamboat. I told my cousin Jim, that's him over yonder." She pointed across the bar at the man who had ridden the snubbing horse and helped her during the rodeo. "I told Jim, 'Now there's a hand. I got to meet that feller.'"

Hewey was stunned into silence. If her looks hadn't first done it, her brash demeanor would have.

"Let's have a drink, partner, then maybe we can have a dance or two." She turned her head barely and spit toward the floor, hitting a man on the leg. He didn't notice.

"After that, well, we might find somethin' else fun to do." Bertha winked at him, then leered.

Hewey heard Wilson behind him, trying to stifle his giggles. Wilson got himself under control and told Bertha, "Yes, ma'am. Hewey here saw you ride earlier and wanted nothin' more than to meet you." He elbowed Hewey in the ribs.

Hewey recovered enough to speak, and he felt sober all of a sudden. "That's right, ma'am. I just wanted to tell you what a good job you done. Pretty ridin', for sure. I appreciate your offer on the dancin', but we was just leavin'."

"Hell, cowboy, it's early. There ain't no need to rush off."

"Well, Miss Simmons, while I'm tempted by your company, I'm a married man. I best not put myself in a tempting situation, but thank you all the same."

Bertha was unbothered. Hewey wasn't the only prospect in the room. "Okay, cowboy. Your loss."

Hewey turned and hurried for the door, Wilson struggling to keep up and laugh at the same time.

"Hold on, Hewey," he said as they walked outside. He could barely talk for the giggles. "I've known you for what, two, three months now? How come you never told me you were married?"

CHAPTER FOURTEEN

Hanley Baker took a little more time heading back to Laramie. His mind felt like hurrying but his body demanded a slower pace. But it gave him plenty of time to think over the situation. The more he thought about it, the more he worried for young Bobby Wilson. His mind kept returning to the hope that he could keep Wilson safe until they hit a fortunate turn.

"Dammit!" Baker slammed the newspaper against his leg.

Several patrons in the café where he was having breakfast looked up, startled. The expression on Baker's face discouraged any comment, though. He had been casually reading the *Cheyenne Daily Leader* when he saw Bob Wilson listed as third place winner in the bucking and pitching contest, followed by a paragraph on the spectacular failed attempt to ride Steamboat by West Texas cowboy Hugh Calloway.

If I saw it, Murphy probably saw it, Baker said to himself. It meant the game had taken a new turn, and he wasn't sure where that turn would lead. This childish stunt would hurt them, he was certain, and he had an idea who was behind it.

I just hope those two will have the good sense to get back to Laramie and keep their eyes open. But right now I wouldn't put money on it.

He found Hewey and Wilson both at the blacksmith shop when he rode in early that afternoon. By that time he had worked his horse into a series of lathers and himself into a foul humor, most of it rightly directed at Hewey, who would have been off riding a colt somewhere had he known Baker was coming and primed to give a chewing.

"What the hell did you think you were doing?" Baker demanded. He gave Wilson a chilling look but directed his wrath at Hewey.

"Aw, Baker, we were just havin' some fun," Hewey answered sheepishly.

"That fun may get somebody killed, and he's sittin' right there." Baker stabbed a finger in Wilson's direction. "I felt like we were going in the right direction before this harebrained stunt, but now I don't know. I'm going to ride through town and see if there's any sign of Murphy, and you two stay put in the camp. Do you understand? No gallivantin' around, no sightseein', no nothin'."

"We will, Mr. Baker," said Wilson. "I promise you that."

"I don't doubt you. It's your runnin' mate there that I have doubts about. If Hewey tries to drag you into somethin' again, just let him go his own way. He's in no danger. You're the one Murphy's after. Remember that. You're the one with a target on your back."

"Yes, sir, and I can feel it itching," Wilson answered.

"Good," Baker retorted. "Let's keep it that way."

Hewey opened his mouth to say something but thought better of it.

Two passes through the main thoroughfares of Laramie showed no sign of either Murphy or Booker, and Baker's foul mood eased. When he returned to the blacksmith shop he found Wilson again helping Thomas, who told him Hewey was in the back riding one of the young horses.

"I hired ol' Hewey to put just a few rides on them broncs," Thomas said. "But ever' day he keeps showin' up and saddling them. He's doing a heck of a job and I'm not paying him much, so I guess I'll just let him go on as long as he wants."

Baker laughed. "Hewey's a damned good hand, if you can keep him out of trouble, which ain't always easy. He'll be leaving soon. That's his way."

"I know it. I've known men like him before. Afraid moss will grow on them if they sit still too long." Thomas lowered his voice so Wilson couldn't hear him. "I tell you something though. I wish Bobby here wouldn't go with y'all when you leave out. He's damned good help, and I need it anymore. He reminds me so much of my son, but I can't tell if that's real or just in my head."

"Yes, sir, I know what you mean," Baker said, although he really did not.

Hewey rode up to the corral on Thomas's dun colt. Baker stood watching, noting the quiet and relaxed manner in which the dun moved. Hewey had it following his subtle cues willingly and not out of any sort of fear.

There was some leftover tension between Hewey and Baker. "You've made a good bit of progress with them," Baker said finally.

"They're nice colts," Hewey replied. "They're ready for a real job, though."

"Come on up to camp. Wilson's cookin' supper, and we've got to talk about some things."

Hewey gave his friend a quizzical look, but Baker didn't say more.

Wilson was bent over their makeshift rock grill when they walked up.

"I hear you two been eating Mrs. Thomas's cookin' more than your own since I've been gone," Baker said.

Wilson looked sheepish then smiled. "I'm trying not to wear out our welcome, but I was about to starve, trying to live on Hewey's cookin'. He can't cook a decent pan of biscuits to save his life."

"I don't remember you givin' it a try," Hewey countered.

"That's because if I did you would find out what a really sorry biscuit tasted like," Wilson said. "No, I'd rather make fun of your biscuits."

"So, Baker, what'd you find out in Green Ridge? Is Bobby here the bank robber or not?"

"Well, it looks like Bobby just may be innocent, but the hard part is going to be keepin' him alive and out of jail long enough to prove it. The marshal back in Green Ridge is at least lookin' at it with an open mind now. He might not exactly believe you're innocent, but he's not certain you're guilty, either."

"So what happens now?" Wilson asked. "What am I supposed to do?"

"I wish I had a good answer. All I know is to keep you out of trouble 'til we figure out something better," Baker answered. "The worst trouble is almost sure to come from Murphy. His voice was the second one at that bank, I'm certain of it. Pinkerton or not, he bears watchin'. The way I see it, you two need to go one direction and I need to draw Murphy off the other way. Maybe that will give us time."

"How do you intend to draw him off, Mr. Baker?" Wilson asked.

"I'm still workin' on that," Baker replied.

"When I needed to get a cow to follow me," Hewey said, "I'd carry the one thing she'd be sure to want—her calf."

"I ain't nobody's calf," Wilson fired back.

"No, but maybe Baker can pass himself off as somethin' else Murphy wants," Hewey suggested.

"What he wants is me," Wilson said somberly.

"What if he thinks somebody else is gonna get to you first?" Hewey asked.

"Sounds like you've got somethin' in mind," Baker said.

"Yeah, but I don't know what it is," Hewey said with his crooked grin. "That's as far as I can get."

Baker sat nodding his head, agreeing with Hewey. "Maybe I can get the rest of the way," Baker said. "Murphy wants you dead before you can spill the frijoles about the bank robbery, and the only way he can be sure about that is to do it himself. What if he's afraid somebody else will get to you before he does?"

"Who would do that, Mr. Baker?" Wilson asked.

"A bounty hunter," Hewey and Baker said in unison. The

two of them looked at each other as if their counterpart had grown an extra head.

Baker grinned and shook his head. "Hewey, you and me have been hangin' around together way too long."

"Murphy doesn't know Hewey or me are here," he continued. "Hell, he doesn't hardly know I exist. He saw me in the saloon in Silverton, but that was it. The two of you hightail it one way, and I'll go the other way as a bounty hunter."

Everyone was silent, thinking about it, before Wilson looked up. "There ain't a bounty on me, though, not that I know of."

"There is now. I forgot to tell you. The marshal in Green Ridge sent it out all over. You're worth a hundred dollars, cash money."

The air went out of Wilson with the news. He just sat, staring at the ground.

Baker went on. "All I need to do is be sure that enough people know I'm around. I'll go around asking questions, talking to the local law. This little scheme won't work if Murphy doesn't hear that there's a bounty hunter prowlin' around and lookin' for the same man he is."

Hewey poked the fire with a slim stick, wondering just how he had become involved in all this. Back in Texas things seemed simpler. He punched some cows, drew a paycheck, had some fun. He wondered if he should go back.

"I'm going toward Cheyenne first. You two made enough noise there to draw Murphy. That man may not be a deacon, but he seems to know what he's doing. He won't be far away, I guarantee you."

"Whatever you think is best," Wilson said.

"I also think you'll have to leave here. It's too public, if Murphy gets anywhere close."

Hewey had been feeling the itch to move on already.

Wilson saw the logic, but the idea saddened him even further. "I guess you're right, but I sort of hate to go."

"You two are gonna have to stay out of trouble," Baker admonished. "The last thing we need is for you to call attention to yourselves."

"What kinda trouble could we get into?" Hewey asked.

"About a dozen different kinds, I suspect," Baker said. "As touchy as things could get, we need someplace to meet."

Baker thought for a moment. "I tell you what, I can't think of a better place than the little town where my niece teaches school. They call it Harmony. It's small enough you can know what's goin' on. Tomorrow mornin' before I head out I'll ride down there, and we'll find a place you can hide out.

"I might ought to introduce you to Daisy. She could be your ears in town, if need be. Hewey, you already met her though, didn't you?"

"Yeah, we met over a snarlin' mountain lion," Hewey said with his crooked grin. "Thank goodness it was somethin' nice and normal like that . . . and not a camel."

Bobby Wilson knocked on the front door of the Thomas house a few minutes after sunrise. Hewey and Baker stood behind him, none looking forward to the upcoming conversation.

Martha Thomas opened the door, smiling broadly when she saw Wilson standing there. Like her husband, she was very taken with him.

"Good morning, Bobby," she said, then smiled at Hewey and Baker. "Come in, everyone. Let me fix you some breakfast."

"Thank you, ma'am, but we've already eaten," Wilson said. "We need to talk to both of you for a few minutes."

Thomas sat studying them from the kitchen table. He had a cup of coffee in front of him, and he gestured to the table. He knew something was awry.

The three sat. Unasked, Martha brought each a cup of coffee, then sat down herself.

Wilson cleared his throat, obviously uncomfortable. "I need to tell you something, both of you. I haven't told you before because I didn't want you to think less of me."

Martha was next to Wilson, and she placed a hand on his in a motherly gesture. "What is it, Bobby?"

It took half an hour to lay out the story. Martha dabbed at

tears several times throughout. Thomas was silent but attentive, taking in all of it.

"Well, we believe you, don't we, Harold?"

Thomas sat rubbing his knuckles, which ached more and more every morning. He looked hard at Wilson. "Yes, I do. You work side by side with a man like we've been doing, and you get a feel for them. I cannot believe you'd ever rob a bank."

Thomas smiled just a little. "Plus, why in the hell would he stay here for two weeks shoeing horses instead of running?"

Wilson had been worried the old couple would doubt him, and he was visibly relieved. "I appreciate what you've done for us. I want you to know that."

Thomas stood and offered one of his big hands. "Son, you get this worked out and then you come back here. I'd like to talk to you about something." He turned to Hewey and Baker. "I'm counting on you two to get him out of this, but if you need anything, anything at all, you ask. I'll come running."

✦

"Hello the camp!" Baker called out. The three of them had found a secluded spot about a mile outside the town of Harmony, then Baker rode into town to see his niece.

"Come on in," Hewey replied as he stepped out from a screen of trees.

"I've brought company," Baker said. He was leading the ill-mannered little mule, and riding at his side was his niece, Daisy.

"I want Daisy to know where to find you if need be," Baker answered. "She also needs to meet Bobby."

Bob Wilson emerged from the trees, caught a glimpse of Daisy Baker, and swept his hat away, something Hewey had failed to do.

"Daisy," Baker said, "this is Bob Wilson."

"I'm happy to meet you, Mr. Wilson," she replied with a broad smile. "I understand you're not really a bank robber."

"No, ma'am, but your uncle is one of the few people who seems to realize that."

"Add me to the list," she said. "I have a lot of faith in Uncle Hanley's judgment."

"You could sure do worse," Wilson agreed.

"I need one of you to take Daisy back to town once I ride out of here," Baker said.

"I'd be happy to do it," Wilson volunteered quickly.

"Nah, that'd best be me," Hewey offered. "Wilson doesn't need to be showin' his face any more than necessary."

"For once I agree with you," Baker said. "Just be sure you come straight back."

"Aw, you're hurtin' my feelings," Hewey said with a grin. "When have I done anything to deserve that?"

"I can give you a list," Baker answered. "Loan me a stub pencil and I'll write it out."

Hewey turned to Daisy. "Your uncle is downright cantankerous."

"Yes, but I love him all the same," she said.

"You have a kind and forgiving soul, ma'am," Hewey replied, again with his crooked grin.

"I'm going to leave you youngsters here to sort things out," Baker said. "I need to be on the trail, and it's late already." He waved his hat and turned westward, letting the big bay pick his own pace. It was a long, smooth trot.

"When do you want to start back?" Hewey asked Daisy. "If we leave now, we can be in Harmony before dark."

"I'm not in any hurry," she replied. "I brought a bedroll, so a day or two, maybe three, will be soon enough."

"We would enjoy your company," Bob Wilson offered.

"I don't know," Hewey began, "a woman in a camp with two men . . ."

"I bake a decent pan of biscuits," Daisy said.

"Well, in that case . . ." Hewey backtracked.

◆❖◆

Hewey and Wilson gathered deadfall timber for the campfire, and Wilson made the most of that evening, helping Daisy with her cooking and finding her a comfortable spot on a short log Hewey had snaked up to the camp with Biscuit. He had gone to the trouble of bringing the log so he could sit on it. Now Wilson and Daisy shared it and he was out his seat.

Wilson's extra effort and attention to Daisy did not escape Hewey's attention. It was irritating, but he weighed it and the prospect of losing Daisy's cooking, mostly the biscuits. The biscuits came out on top, and he said nothing.

What he did not consider at first was the effect that Wilson's attentions produced in Daisy. She was smiling and blushing, and she never looked away from Wilson except for those moments when Hewey thought she was acting coy. As the evening wore on, Daisy sidled up closer and closer to Wilson, so close that Hewey thought he might get his old seat back on the log. The next thing Hewey knew, Daisy had her head on Wilson's shoulder.

Hewey knew very little of jealousy when it came to women, given that most of those he had known were strictly temporary and mostly commercial attractions. Thus he was uncertain what he was feeling as he watched Daisy and Wilson. All he knew was that it made him uncomfortable.

Nevertheless, he couldn't stop watching until he began to feel like an intruder. Even then he would hazard the occasional glance.

"I don't mean to get in the way," Hewey eventually said. "But I've heard somethin' about biscuits, and so far I ain't seen any biscuits, smelled any biscuits, or tasted any biscuits."

Wilson gave him a frown and Daisy laughed. "We'll have biscuits soon," she promised.

Hewey enjoyed the pretty laugh and looked forward to the biscuits. He ignored Wilson's frown.

CHAPTER
FIFTEEN

Cheyenne was Hanley Baker's first major destination, but he intended to stop at any little town or even the occasional country store he found, so rather than ride due east cross-country he followed the road back to Laramie and then took the road southeast toward Cheyenne. It added time, but his goal was to talk to people and be seen, not to get there fast.

He stopped at a town called Buford, which was situated along the railroad and also the road to Cheyenne. It was a bustling town with signs of progress. There was an abandoned fort but a brand-new school.

The clerk of a small dry goods store where he stopped to purchase a few supplies studied Baker a moment when Baker asked if he had seen anyone fitting Wilson's description.

"I don't like to butt into another fella's business, but it strikes me that a man came through here yesterday and bought pretty much the same sort of traveling supplies you're buying now," said the store clerk. "He asked about this same young fella but couldn't give a good enough description for me to tell him yea or nay. Don't suppose you're looking for the same young man."

Hanley was surprised to find Murphy so close and so soon. He had assumed the detective would be nearby, but this was close, too close.

"Sounds like we're after the same man, sure does," Baker said. "Was this feller a bounty hunter, too?"

He knew that was getting close to dishonesty but felt it was not quite there. He planned to stay straight if he could. It might help them all in the future.

The clerk rubbed his short pencil against his cheek. "I don't rightly know. Seems he said he was a detective of some sort." He leaned toward Baker and whispered, "He wasn't a very friendly sort, if you know what I mean."

"Yes, sir, I do. It's a shame, too. Folks act like that more and more, don't they?"

Although they were alone in the store, the clerk looked around to see if anyone was listening, then agreed. "Especially the young ones."

"One more thing, sir, then I'll get out of your way," Baker said. "Was this feller alone, or was there someone with him?"

The clerk was enjoying the conversation, and Baker could tell it. The man probably gossiped with anyone who would listen. That was just what he needed.

"Well," said the clerk. "He came in alone, but there was another man, sort of a heavyset man if you know what I mean. Well, he stayed outside. I don't know why. I have a nice store, in my opinion."

Baker had paid before he began his questions, so he gathered his few supplies and headed for the door. As he opened it, he turned back. "Say, did you see which direction they rode when they left here?"

"That I cannot tell you. Another customer came in, sort of a suspicious-looking type, if you know what I mean. I had to keep my eyes on him."

Baker nodded at the man. "Thank you for the help."

He patted the little mule on the neck after he had loaded the few supplies in the panniers. He couldn't understand how Hewey could be so good with horses but have such an issue with Little Jim. He shook his head side to side, thinking about it.

Baker reined his big bay southeast toward Cheyenne. If Murphy had visited the store the day before, that meant he was out in front of Baker somewhere. That gave him a little peace, knowing Murphy wasn't likely to run up behind him.

It also meant he needed to keep his eyes open and not run up behind Murphy. The big bay could cover ground easily, and Little Jim the mule could get his short legs into a mile-eating long trot when necessary.

The plan was for Murphy to follow him, but it was still early and he would take the lead somewhere down the road. Baker was watchful, assuming he might be narrowing the small gap with Murphy. Baker had an advantage in that he knew the game he was playing and Murphy did not. It was nevertheless a small advantage because Murphy obviously knew what he was doing. The man was no fool, and Baker knew he had best keep that in mind.

Hewey Calloway's jealousy over the budding relationship between Wilson and Daisy Baker was dissipating with every meal she prepared. She had followed through on her promise of biscuits the first evening, and the next morning the breakfast was as good as Hewey could ever remember, and he was a fan of a good breakfast.

"Daisy, how would you like to go to Canada?" he asked, lounging against his bedroll, which was propped against the new log he had snaked up with Biscuit while Daisy was cooking breakfast. "That's where I'm headed, and I'm gonna be so spoilt to your cookin' that I may not be able to go without you."

Daisy beamed. "Thank you, Hewey." She turned to Wilson. "Bob, you're not going to Canada, are you?"

"Daisy, I don't have any plans further than a day or two out. I've been takin' it day by day ever' since this deal began. But no, I don't plan to go to Canada, unless it's to run from the law."

Wilson did not seem to notice Daisy's fear that he might be leaving, but Hewey did. A little bit more of the jealousy washed away and was replaced by relief. He had seen his brother, Walter, told many times by his wife, Eve, where he could or could not go, and Hewey wanted no part of that sort of arrangement.

The next morning while Wilson helped Daisy with the breakfast dishes she told him she planned to ride into town that morning. "I need to get a couple things from my house, and I want to cook you two something special tonight. I've always wanted to cook an apple cobbler on a fire like a real wagon cook, but I've really never had the opportunity. I'm going to try it today, and I need to buy a few things."

"I'd be happy to ride in with you," Wilson said immediately.

"No, you stay here, out of sight. It's only a mile. I'll be perfectly fine."

Wilson looked at Hewey, hoping for an ally. "Nope, I ain't getting' in this deal."

※

"Miss Baker, do you know a man by the name of Murphy?" asked the young clerk at the Harmony Mercantile. Daisy had ridden by her small house and picked up the few items she had forgotten, then rode over to the town's only store.

"He was asking around about you, and something in his demeanor gave me pause, so I dodged his question. I told him I'm new around here and haven't met everyone yet. I hope I did the right thing."

Daisy blanched, obviously shaken. She had assumed Murphy was many miles away. The clerk saw the effect his words had and became concerned. "Are you okay, Ms. Baker?"

"Yes, I'm sorry. I just felt a little faint for a moment there. You did precisely the right thing, Mr. Barnes," she replied without trying to hide the quaver in her voice. "I had hoped never to meet Mr. Murphy, but I do know who he is."

"Is there anything I can do to help?" asked Barnes.

"Thank you, but you've already been more help than you can know," Daisy Baker said.

※

"Bob! Hewey! Mr. Murphy is in town! We have to leave here. Now!"

"Murphy? How did he find us?" Wilson asked incredulously.

"He's a detective, just like Baker," Hewey answered. "It's his job to find people, and we can't be too surprised that he's good at it. Now we better travel. I just don't know where to go so Baker can find us and Murphy can't."

Daisy looked at Wilson, then took his hand in hers. "I think the best thing for you to do, really the only thing for you to do, is turn yourself in."

"What?" Wilson asked, shock in his voice.

"That's not somethin' I'd usually suggest," Hewey piped in by way of agreement. "But in this case it might be just the ticket."

Wilson was still shaking his head. "They'll hang me if I do. Murphy and Booker will pin it on me, then they'll hang me."

"That could be," Hewey allowed. "But if you stay out here, Murphy is going to kill you. I saw it in his eyes. He's got no problem with it, and that would be the simplest way to get rid of you."

"Please, Bob," Daisy implored.

"Where, in Harmony?" Wilson asked.

"There is no jail or sheriff in Harmony."

Hewey snapped his fingers. "We'll go to Laramie. Remember the sheriff there? Darnall. He seemed like a decent feller. He'll at least make them wait for a trial before they hang you."

"That's comforting, Hewey," Daisy said icily.

"I'll start saddlin' them ponies. You two gather our stuff. We better travel right now!"

Hewey felt they needed Baker's help in this situation, and no one disagreed with him. He considered sending Wilson and Daisy to Laramie alone and heading due east, cutting cross-country to Cheyenne, where he knew Baker had been headed.

"I'm going with you to Laramie," he said when they had the horses saddled and their belongings packed. "I know the sheriff better than you, and what if we run into Murphy on the way there?"

Daisy wheeled her paint horse northward through the trees, eager to be off. She was frightened, not for herself but for Wilson. "Yes, please come with us, Hewey. But either way, you two *hurry up!*"

Hewey looked at Wilson, raised his eyebrows and grinned, then nudged Biscuit into a trot behind the paint.

It was twenty miles into Laramie. They put their horses in a trot and kept them there. Biscuit and Wilson's gray were hard from steady riding, and they could trot nearly all day. Daisy's paint had been standing around eating most of the time, and it was suffering by the time they reached town.

The trip was uneventful aside from one scare when the trio met two riders coming toward them on the road. From a distance the men looked as if they could have been Murphy and the banker Booker.

"Everybody stay ready," Hewey told them. "If need be, you two cut south toward the river. I'll slow them down best I can, then we'll meet in Laramie."

Wilson didn't like it. "I won't leave you to fight while I run."

"Yes, you will," Daisy said. "Murphy is after you. He doesn't care about Hewey."

The gap between them and the oncoming riders closed before Wilson could argue further. He and Hewey both kept their hands near their rifle scabbards, but neither drew them. Hewey wished for the pistol that was in his saddlebags. He didn't even own a holster, so that was the only place he could carry it. It was uncomfortable to carry the revolver in his waistband while walking around and downright impossible while on a horse.

The tension eased as they drew nearer and realized the two riders were complete strangers.

"I got to get back to Texas, back to punchin' cows," Hewey told Wilson and Daisy. "I'm not cut out for the outlaw life. I can't handle the tension."

It was late in the afternoon when they rode up to the blacksmith shop. Hewey thought it would be a good idea if Mr. Thomas went with them to the sheriff's office to vouch for Wilson, and the others agreed. They found Thomas sitting outside his shop, done for the day and evidently watching traffic go by, what little there was. He brightened when he saw them coming.

"I sure didn't expect to see y'all back so soon. I thought you were hiding from the law, not out pickin' up women." He grinned and tipped his hat to Daisy. "Harold Thomas, ma'am. Nice to meet you."

"Mr. Thomas, I need your help," Wilson said, urgency in his voice. "That detective was in Harmony yesterday. I'm scared of what will happen if he finds me. I want to turn myself in, but I'd like for you to talk to your friend Darnall and see if he'll help me."

"Of course I'll help. You want to go now?"

"I think we'd better," Wilson said. "I don't know where Murphy is right now."

"Well, let's go." Thomas set off at a walk. Wilson stepped off and offered his horse to the older man. "Thank you, son, but that gray of yours is too damn tall."

Wilson stayed on the ground, walking beside Thomas and leading his horse. Daisy and Hewey rode behind, both watchful of the crowd as they rode into town.

<hr />

"Hell, I've known for nearly two weeks that somethin' was up with this boy," the sheriff told Thomas. "He got so damn nervous that morning when he realized I was the sheriff, and then I got a wanted poster for a man that fit his description. Didn't have no picture, but I thought it might be him."

"Why didn't you do anything, Tom?" asked Thomas, who was sitting in a chair across the desk from the sheriff. Hewey, Wilson, and Daisy all stood behind, crowded into the small room.

"Well, he was a friend of Hewey here. Hewey's a good ol' boy, but that didn't mean too much to me, really." The sheriff paused, not knowing how to say what was on his mind. "I went back out to your shop a few days ago to talk to Bob. The two of you were inside but didn't see me. I watched you for a minute. You were lookin' at him like he was *your* Bobby, and I didn't have the heart to interfere. I sneaked off without you knowing I was even there."

Thomas stared at his friend, then looked down at his big hands. "Thank you, Tom," he said finally.

Everyone was quiet, not knowing what to say. Hewey tried to think of a joke but couldn't.

Darnall finally went on. "Wilson, if you want to do this then I'm going to do it right. I'm going to arrest you proper and lock you in the jail. There is a warrant out for your arrest, and you just admitted you are this same Bob Wilson."

The color was draining from Wilson's face. He began to wonder if he had made a mistake.

"Now, I will promise you that I will not turn you over to just anyone who tries to come in here and take you. I am the chief law enforcement officer in Albany County, and I don't give a damn what some Pinkerton detective says. If the sheriff out of Colorado shows up with a court order, then I'll have to turn you over to him. But I'll make certain it's square first."

"That's all we ask, Tom," Thomas said.

CHAPTER SIXTEEN

Hewey Calloway left Laramie before dawn, riding Biscuit and leading two of Thomas's young horses, the sorrel and the dun. He had considered leaving for Cheyenne the night before, but it was almost dark by the time they left the sheriff's office. Daisy and Thomas persuaded him to wait.

The sorrel and dun led fine at a walk and trot but refused to hit a lope. Hewey finally pulled down his rope and placed the loop over the sorrel's hip, letting it dangle to just above the hocks.

When the sorrel declined to lope, he pulled the rope. The sorrel didn't like the loop tightening around its hind legs, so it sped up. The dun came with it, and Hewey and all three horses went down the road as the sun came up over the hills in front of them.

It was fifty miles to Cheyenne, give or take, and Hewey switched horses twice, riding all three for a stretch. He would lope a mile or two, then trot a mile or so, then back to a lope, all day long. Wilson was locked in the jail, but Hewey felt an urgency to find Baker and get back with help.

◆◈◆

The rodeo was over and the crowd gone home when Hanley Baker reached Cheyenne. He found the sheriff's office but was told by an attractive older lady at the front desk that the sheriff takes a few days recuperation time after the rodeo. A town full of drunk cowboys and rodeo fans is hard on both the sheriff's body and mind, she said. He was gone fishing.

The lady wore more makeup and was showing more of her chest than was customary for the time and place, and she kept smiling suggestively at Baker. "Is there something *I* can help you with, sugar?"

Baker began to feel a little warm. He could feel a few sweat droplets forming under his hat. He could not understand how it got so hot so suddenly, and in Wyoming. "Yes, ma'am. Could be. I'm lookin' for a wanted man, name of Bob Wilson. He won a little money here last week in the bronc ridin'."

"Oh honey, all I know about him is that he seems to have left town. Only way I know that is there was a detective in here the other day talking to Troy—that's the sheriff—about this Wilson character. Troy told him as far as he knows this fellow had left town."

"Do you happen to remember the name of this detective?" Baker asked.

"I never heard that, sugar. He was a rude sort of fellow and I didn't care to talk to him any more than I had to."

"Thank you, ma'am. I appreciate all the help."

"Quitting time around here is in about an hour, honey. If you're not in a hurry we could go get a drink, or something."

Baker wasn't sure whether to accept or take off running. "I better keep travelin', ma'am. Got some folks countin' on me."

"Well, you get that taken care of, you just come on back," she said. "We might do something to get the law after *us*."

※

The sun was getting low when Hewey rode into Cheyenne.

His horses were tired, and so was he. The town was empty compared to his last visit. He didn't have much of a plan and could not decide whether to wait for Baker or to ride on if he didn't happen to find him in town.

He rode slowly down the main street, looking for Baker's big bay among the horses tied outside the various businesses. It was late enough in the day that the establishments that kept early hours were already closed for the day. The only things open were the saloons and cafés.

The majority of the businesses were located along one main road, and Hewey found no sign of Baker's bay along it. He rode a block in each direction, looking up and down the roads. There was nothing promising anywhere.

Discouraged, Hewey rode back to a livery stable he had passed earlier. It was too dark to find a spot outside town to stake the horses. A boy at the livery barn showed him an outside pen where he could keep the horses for cheaper than an inside stall. The horses weren't used to much luxury anyway.

The boy went for some hay. Hewey unsaddled the dun, then led all three together toward the pen. He passed a horse eating some grass hay from a feeder, then stopped and turned back. It was Baker's big bay, and on the other side of it stood the little gray mule.

"I'll be derned," said Hewey, his spirits lifting.

It took longer to locate Baker than Hewey expected. He had left the livery barn on foot, reasoning that Baker would not have gone far on foot himself. The first two saloons he came to held no old Rangers. Hewey allowed himself one beer in the first. It had been a long day, he rationalized.

Baker was not in the little café next door to the second saloon. Hewey considered ordering. He hadn't eaten a thing since breakfast early that morning, and he was feeling gaunt. Deciding it would take too much time, he went on.

Two doors down was a hotel, but Hewey had never seen Baker in a hotel so he didn't bother to go inside. Striding down the plank sidewalk, he saw something out of the corner of his eye and stopped suddenly.

The hotel had a small restaurant on the first floor, an upscale sort of establishment with a formal dining room. There were several windows looking out into the street, and sitting near one of them was Baker, along with a shiny lady a decade younger than he was. Baker was smiling and talking, obviously enjoying himself.

"You old scoundrel," Hewey said to himself, then headed inside. A haughty-looking man at the hotel's front desk looked down his long nose at Hewey and asked if he could be of any service. Hewey felt like the man would prefer that service to be showing him the exit.

"Just meetin' a friend." Hewey grinned at him. "But I might be back for a room if I don't find a hotel that's not so run-down." The clerk glared, and Hewey walked on into the dining area.

Baker was so enthralled in his conversation and his companion that he never saw Hewey coming.

"Hard at it, I see," Hewey said loudly.

The shock was evident in Baker's eyes, and this time it was he who needed a few seconds to trust his eyes. Hewey was not supposed to be there. The lady looked on with amusement in her brown eyes.

"What the hell are you doin' here?" Baker growled finally. "I thought I'd made it clear that you were supposed to keep an eye on Bobby and not go gallivantin' around the country."

"And I kinda thought you were enough Ranger that you wouldn't get skunked by a Pinkerton. That sumbitch Murphy is in Harmony. Or he was yesterday at least."

"I'll be damned."

"There's a good chance of that eventually," Hewey chuckled.

Baker's female companion cleared her throat gently, then held out her hand to Hewey. "I'm Samantha Dearing. You must be the Hewey Calloway that Hanley has been talking about."

Hewey tipped his hat, trying not to look at the freckles showing where he shouldn't be looking. He understood how Baker could have gotten off course. "Nice to meet you, ma'am."

"Well don't blush, sugar," she teased. "Hanley here has already done enough of that to last us the night."

"Yes, ma'am, it's just . . ."

"Don't you dare, Hewey," Baker growled.

Dearing laughed in a beautiful, husky way, and Baker and Hewey both grinned like fools. "Please join us, Mr. Calloway."

"He's fine. I'm sure he's already eaten." Baker glared forcefully at Hewey, who missed it entirely because he was staring at Dearing again.

"Thank you, ma'am. I'm starved."

"So what brings you here, Mr. Calloway? Hanley has regaled me with stories of your current situation, but as I understood it you were many miles away in the company of your friend."

Hewey gave Baker a confused look. He couldn't quite get a handle on the situation. Samantha Dearing dressed much like a saloon girl, a high-end one at that, but she was too old for that business. And then she spoke like an English teacher. He had never seen anything like it and got the feeling Baker hadn't, either.

"Well," he said finally. "Wilson's in jail in Laramie and it's up to us to either get him out or make sure he stays in."

"What the hell are you talkin' about?" demanded Baker. "You're not makin' a whole lot of sense."

"It was your niece's idea," Hewey explained. "But it was a good one. She rode into Harmony to the store, and Murphy had just been there. I don't guess he followed you at all."

"So did Wilson get arrested, or did he turn himself in?" asked Dearing, who was following the conversation with interest.

"Yes, ma'am, he turned himself in. It was Daisy's idea. That's Baker's niece. She figured it was the only place he'd be safe, and maybe Baker could figure out some way to prove he was innocent before it's too late."

Baker smiled, approving of the plan. It sounded like there had not been a better choice. "Smart girl. She takes after her uncle."

"I just hope we can get her uncle to quit socializin' long enough to help."

"Shut up, Hewey."

Dearing laughed her husky laugh again, and they both swooned.

Hewey and Baker were waiting outside the café nearest the livery barn when it opened the next morning. Their horses and the little mule were tied outside, ready to travel.

Baker was quiet, not quite grouchy. Hewey would have called it melancholy if he had known what the word meant. "Why are you so derned quiet?" he finally asked between big bites. It was his type of café. The waitress wasn't exactly friendly, but at least she wasn't rude, like the one in the hotel the night before.

"You got to promise not to give me a hard time if I tell you."

"Why, I never teased nobody in my whole life." Hewey tried to grin but his mouth was full. Baker did not return the humor. "All right, yes, I promise not to give you a hard time."

Baker sighed. "I don't know what it is, Hewey. I know we got to go see what we can do for Wilson, but I don't want to leave. I'd rather stay here and see Samantha again. I can't get her out of my mind."

"I been meaning to ask you about her," Hewey said. "Is she some kind of professional lady or what?"

"Dammit, Hewey! She works at the sheriff's office." Baker's face turned red instantly.

"Easy now. I'm sorry," Hewey said. "She didn't act nothin' like a saloon girl, but you know, she sort of looks like one, in a good kind of way."

"Just shut up, will you?"

CHAPTER SEVENTEEN

They found Tom Darnall sitting at his desk inside the sheriff's office back in Laramie. They had alternated horses all day long, rode them hard and made it to town just before dusk.

"Between what I've heard from Miss Baker and what I've read in the newspapers, I think I have a pretty good idea what that bank robbery was all about," Darnall told Baker. "Good enough, at least, to give you a hand. If I'm wrong, it won't kill anybody before I figure it out."

"That's good to hear," Baker said, "because Hewey and I need to spend some time tracking down Murphy and Booker, and it sure would be easier to do if we knew Bob Wilson was safe in one of your cells."

"He'll be as safe as anybody can be, in a cell without a window. About the only thing more I could do is give him a pistol, and I can't see going that far."

"Wouldn't ask you to," Baker replied. "Besides, he doesn't carry one, so I'm not even sure he could use it."

Baker studied Darnall, wondering where the man's line was. "If I could find Murphy and Booker and get them here, would you hold them and question them? I just can't see any other way for this to break. Nothing new is coming to the surface. We need them to talk, somehow."

Darnall rubbed his temples, thinking about that. "I like you boys, but I cannot in good conscience approve of one citizen hunting down another and bringing him into my jail, even if you could get that done peacefully. Now, since you were a Texas Ranger I *could* see fit to deputize you. And since I have a wanted bank robber in my jail and these men seem to be material witnesses at the very least, it would tickle me if my deputy could bring them here for a few questions."

Baker nodded his head, grateful for the assistance. "How about Hewey? You gonna deputize him, too?"

"No, just you. Hewey's a good ol' boy, but I'm not sure he's law enforcement material."

Baker smiled, remembering Hewey's actions in Colorado the year before. "I know what you mean, but he just might surprise you."

The next morning Baker and Hewey checked in early with Darnall. They had already decided that Murphy was sure to be coming and might already be in the vicinity. The best bet, they thought, was to find him first.

"If it suits you, Sheriff," Baker said, "we're just going to look around town some. If that doesn't turn up anything we'll scout around farther out. I don't know what else to do, do you?"

The sheriff shook his head. "No, I don't. But I cannot see a Pinkerton detective coming in here after Bob Wilson. It's just too reckless."

"Do we even know this feller is a Pinkerton man?" asked Hewey.

"I sent a telegraph yesterday to their main office," said Darnall. "Haven't heard anything back yet."

"Why didn't you call on the telephone?" Hewey asked. "I ain't never used one, but I heard that's the way now."

"I tried, believe it or not. Couldn't get the damn thing to work."

The first day of scouting produced nothing but two tired men and two tired horses. Hewey rode one of Thomas's young horses, so he earned a small paycheck. Baker realized he and Darnall had never discussed pay and that he was probably considered a volunteer.

Baker also realized that although Hewey might have a few shortcomings as far as being a lawman—chiefly lack of desire—he had some other qualities that certainly helped. They had begun asking folks around town and just outside of it if they had seen Murphy and Booker.

Hewey, it turned out, was excellent at describing the men and could even mimic their voices somewhat. They left every questionee laughing and promising to send word should they see the men.

"Hewey, you have more natural talent and ability than nearly anyone I've ever known. You're good at nearly everything, and people naturally just like to be around you. Maybe you ought to consider putting it to better use."

Hewey groaned theatrically. "Oh hell, don't start that again. We were just beginning to get along."

The next day was more of the same. Darnall told them that morning he thought it was pointless, but Hewey and Baker widened their circle and stayed out all day. No one they spoke to had seen anyone resembling Murphy or Booker.

"Miss Baker, could I treat you to supper?" asked Sheriff Darnall that evening. "There's a pretty decent café just around the corner here, and we can bring a plate back for your Mr. Wilson."

While Wilson had not been enjoying his time in jail, he could not complain about the meal service. Breakfast had always been brought by the sheriff from one of two nearby cafés, and either Daisy Baker or Martha Thomas cooked and delivered his dinner and supper. They had even begun to feed the sheriff, as well, which made the unusual jailing arrangement easier for the old lawman to take. He was a single man and slept in the jail. Home cooking was a treat, but so was taking a pretty young girl like Daisy out to the café.

"Why, thank you, Sheriff," Daisy answered. "I'm not too bashful to take you up on a nice meal."

"I didn't say anything about the quality of the food," Darnall cautioned with a smile, "just that the café is decent and handy."

"I'll take my chances," Daisy Baker said.

※

The two had not been in the café more than a few minutes when a man crossed the street and went straight to the jail. Murphy had been hiding and watching for nearly two days for a chance. The sheriff, he had found, had been sticking very close to the jail and his prisoner.

It was early evening and still light outside, which bothered Murphy. He saw no alternative, though, due to the sheriff's habit of remaining nearby.

From his pocket Murphy pulled a small bar. It was built much like a carpenter's nail bar, but Murphy had this one handmade years ago for occasions such as this. The bar was strong and forceful yet small enough to conceal.

The door of the jail could be secured from the inside with a hefty wooden bar, but when there was no one inside it could only be locked with a simple key and sliding bolt. Murphy inserted his small pry bar between the door and jamb, then tugged backward on it. The wooden jamb splintered, and he easily pushed open the door.

The jail was made up of three rooms. The front door opened into the office, which held an old wooden desk and a small wooden table with four chairs. Murphy knew the door opposite that could be barred from the office must hold the jail cells, and he correctly assumed the side door to be a small apartment.

There was one glass window on the front of the jail, and he peeked out it. Satisfied, he moved around behind the desk. He found the keys to the cell doors in the top drawer of Darnall's desk.

Wasting no time or motion, Murphy opened the heavy door to the cell block. Wilson was lying on the cot reading *The Red*

Badge of Courage, which Martha Thomas had loaned him. He had never been an avid reader but was enjoying the story so far. It passed the time, and he'd had plenty of that lately.

He had heard sounds in the office and assumed it was Darnall, who had never been far away. When the door opened he looked up to find a large revolver pointed at him.

"If you yell, I might as well shoot you," Murphy said. "You will come with me quietly or I'll kill you here. Do you understand that?"

Wilson recognized the voice instantly. His mouth had gone dry, and it was difficult to speak. "Yes," he said finally.

The first key turned out to be the wrong one, but the second one turned the cell's simple lock. Murphy swung the door inward and was surprised it didn't creak.

"Put your boots on quick, or you're going barefoot."

Wilson grabbed his boots from under the cot and slid them on. His hat was sitting upside down on the floor, and he put it on also.

"Stand up, slowly, and walk into the front room."

Murphy stepped aside but kept the big pistol pointed at Wilson's middle. Wilson was regaining his composure and had begun to look for an opportunity, but Murphy's gun never wavered. He stopped at the broken front door with Murphy behind him.

"Is your horse at the livery stable?" came Murphy's voice from behind him.

"No. The blacksmith shop."

"What?" Murphy hissed. The answer surprised and irritated him. Wilson didn't answer because he didn't know what to say.

"Okay, we're going to walk down there, side by side, with you on my left. If you make a wrong move or say the wrong thing, I will shoot you where you stand. Now open that door and go."

Murphy holstered his pistol, but he kept his hand on the butt. He stayed as far away from Wilson as the wooden sidewalk would allow. Wilson noticed this and knew an attempt to grab Murphy was likely to end badly for him.

Across the street a heavyset man sat on a big sorrel horse,

watching them. He held the bridle reins to another saddled horse. Wilson had seen him for only a moment back in Green Ridge, but he recognized him as the other man outside the bank.

Booker gave them a short start, then followed slowly behind, keeping himself separate from the two men on foot.

They met two horsemen coming up the street toward them, but it was only teenaged boys who showed them little interest. Toward the edge of town an older couple sat on their front porch as they walked past. Murphy nodded at them congenially, and Wilson kept quiet. He couldn't see how they could help him much.

Wilson had hoped to find Baker and Hewey at Thomas's shop, but the place was deserted. He noticed their horses were gone, and he had no idea where they were. He knew they had been scouting around for Murphy, but he knew nothing of the details.

Thomas, it seemed, had gone home for the evening.

Wilson looked toward the small house, but all was quiet.

Hewey and Baker rode into town as the evening headed toward dark. As they passed one of the small cafés, Sheriff Darnall and Daisy stepped out the front door. Daisy was carrying a plate covered with a white towel.

"Find anything, fellers?" asked the sheriff.

"Nothin' but an empty stomach," replied Hewey, eyeing the plate Daisy carried.

Daisy held up a fist, teasing. "Stay back, Hewey. This is Bob's supper."

"I'm gonna give this ol' pony a drink, then I'm coming right back here."

Darnall and Daisy fell into step with the horses, since they were all headed the same direction. The sheriff stopped when he saw the jail's front door. "What in the hell?"

Daisy dropped the plate and rushed inside. Darnall tried to grab her but missed. Baker was off his horse in an instant, moving faster than anyone thought he could. He followed his niece inside, afraid of what they would find.

Sheriff Darnall was quick to claim responsibility for the jailbreak, if it could even be called a jailbreak. "It was my fault," he insisted. "I should never have left the jail unattended."

"A man's gotta eat sometime," Hewey replied. "Who would have expected Murphy to be so quick to turn a supper break into a jailbreak? Besides, who would expect anybody to break *into* a jail when everybody else is trying to break *out?*"

"We could stand here and argue about it all night long if we had the time," Baker said, "but we don't. As much as it hurts my pride to say it, Hewey's right. There's no blame to throw around, just catchin' up to do. And we'd best be at that."

"How long were you gone?" Baker asked Darnall.

"Not long at all. Maybe twenty, thirty minutes."

"Then they can't have gone far. We'll go to the blacksmith shop for fresh horses. Are you comin' with us?"

"Damn right I'm coming," answered Darnall. "This is my jail, and that was my prisoner. I will not tolerate this."

"Then meet us here as soon as we can all get saddled," Baker said. "Daisy, I want you to stay right here."

"No, I'm going with you as far as the Thomases' house. They're as concerned as any of us and have a right to know what's happened."

Baker looked at Hewey, who just shrugged his shoulders and walked out the door.

Daisy and Baker walked because Baker could not allow himself to ride while his niece had to walk, and she refused to ride his horse if he walked. Hewey thought it all ridiculous and just rode his horse.

Baker looked up at Hewey. "Where's your pistol?"

"It's in my saddlebag. Dern thing pokes me if I get on a horse with it stuck in my britches."

"You better get it out anyway," Baker said. "You'll want it when we catch up to Murphy."

"I'll get it when we swap horses. Don't know how I'm gonna carry it though."

Thomas's small road split just past his entrance, with one lane leading up to his house and the other the blacksmith shop. Daisy turned toward the house.

Baker called after her. "Daisy, please stay here 'til we get back. I can tell you're itching to come, but I couldn't stand it if somethin' happened to you."

"I'll stay, Uncle Hanley, but you have to promise you'll bring Bob back."

Baker hesitated, cringing inside. "I promise. Now go; we have to get moving."

※

It wasn't far—a kid with a good arm could have thrown a rock to where they were headed behind the blacksmith shop, but Baker stepped back on his bay horse rather than walking. Old habits are hard to break, and he wasn't even trying.

The shop was dim and empty as they rode past, with no sign of Thomas. The sun was still up but getting low on the western horizon. They were riding almost side by side, with Hewey slightly in the lead as they rounded the corner of the shop headed for the corral behind.

Hewey pulled up suddenly once they cleared the corner of the building, and a second later Baker saw why. A pudgy man with his back turned to them held a revolver on Wilson, who stood saddling his own gray horse. They were forty feet from Hewey and had not heard them approaching.

Baker pulled his pistol and pointed it at the man. "Drop that pistol, mister, and turn around real slow."

Wilson looked up from his horse, relief on his face. The fat man lowered his gun but did not drop it. He turned slowly and looked at them.

"You'd be Booker, I guess," Baker said.

The banker did not respond. He did not seem as alarmed as he should, Baker thought.

It did not feel right to Hewey, either. He looked around and spotted the reason. "Two horses over there, Baker." He pointed to the two saddled horses tied off to the side, almost out of sight behind a solid fence. "Murphy's here."

"You'd be right," came a voice from behind them. "Get your hands up and dismount. You there, Texas Ranger, you pitch that pistol on the ground."

Hewey saw a sour look on Baker's face; Murphy had suckered him again.

"Go easy, now," Murphy said as they both began to step down from their horses. "It wouldn't bother me none at all to kill you both, as much trouble as you've caused us."

Hewey and Baker both moved slowly, keeping their hands where Murphy could see them.

"Now get over there by the other one," Murphy ordered, a self-satisfied smirk on his face. "This is going to be easier by far than I expected."

Carefully, Hewey and Baker walked around Booker, then stopped near Wilson. All three turned to face Murphy and Booker, who stood side by side near the back wall of the blacksmith shop. Murphy glanced at Booker out of the corner of his eye. "Keep your gun on them and watch them close," he ordered. "Especially that old one."

Booker kept his gun pointed, but he showed neither confidence nor enthusiasm. This part had always been Murphy's job. He was nervous. He had never wanted to search for Wilson himself, but Murphy had forced him.

Baker was seething. He was mad that Murphy had got the best of him again, but he was particularly mad to have a gun pointed at him. He had been shot at multiple times as a Ranger, but he had never been held at gunpoint. He didn't much care for it.

"What are we going to do with them?" Booker asked, his voice almost shaking.

"It depends on how cooperative these fellows care to be. We start shooting right here and we'll have to run for it." Murphy looked right at Baker then. "I think you know where this is headed. We can do it here, right now, or you can ride out of here real quiet and the three of you can live just a little bit longer."

Both Hewey and Baker were about to vote for later when Wilson spoke up. He had been quiet until then, but something broke in the young man when Murphy said he planned to kill all of them. Wilson stepped forward a couple steps and pointed his finger at their captors.

"No, I'm done with all this. You bastards have chased me for months, and I'm through with it."

"Easy Wilson," Hewey cautioned, but the boy showed no sign of hearing.

"I'm done running." His volume had been rising with his temper, and he was almost shouting now. "Shoot me if you want, but we're not going anywhere. I'm done being scared."

Murphy smiled at that. Hewey and Baker saw the gleam in his eye. It looked to them like he *wanted* to shoot them. In the heat of the moment Wilson did not see it, or it just did not register.

From Hewey. "Shut up, Wilson."

Wilson turned his tirade toward Booker. "All this because you stole money from the people who trusted you to protect it. Those poor people in that little town worked harder for that money than you ever have in your life, and you took it from them."

Hewey thought he saw something move at the corner of the building behind Murphy and Booker, but when he looked again there was nothing there. He turned his attention back to the scene quickly escalating in front of him.

"You think you're better than us, I can tell it," Wilson told Booker. "But you're nothing but a thief. A common criminal."

Booker's face was screwing up with rage. He was not accustomed to being spoken to like this, certainly not from some half-grown cowpuncher.

"Dammit, Bob, shut up," Hewey pleaded.

Wilson was having none of it. He saw what he was doing to Booker. "Not only are you just a common, low-life criminal, you're a coward at heart, aren't you, fat man?"

Booker blinked one time, then shot Wilson in the chest. Wilson made a sound that would haunt Hewey for many years to come, and then he fell backward, landing without any attempt to catch himself.

Almost instantly there was movement from behind the corner of the shop. Harold Thomas let out another sound that Hewey would hear in the darkness for years. Thomas screamed "Bobby!" and in that instant Hewey could not tell if he was yelling for Wilson or his own son, Bobby.

Thomas charged at Booker, moving faster than he had in two decades or more. It took him two big steps to cover the short distance to the banker, who began turning but was too slow. Thomas swung his right arm in a wide arc and slapped Booker in the side of the head with the pair of horseshoe tongs he had gone back for after he first saw what was happening behind his shop.

Years and years of swinging heavy hammers and wrestling unruly horses had made a strong man of Thomas, and in his rage he put everything he had into that first swing. It likely killed the banker, but later no one knew for certain because Thomas straddled the fallen banker and hit him with the tongs four more times in the forehead, releasing some inner demon, before he caught himself and stopped.

In the instant Thomas first screamed, Murphy turned his gun toward the charging blacksmith. He was quick enough, but Booker was in the way and blocked any shot. When Booker fell after Thomas's first blow, Murphy momentarily had a clear shot at the enraged blacksmith, who never even looked at him.

It was a sure shot, only half a dozen steps away.

Murphy was tightening the trigger when Hewey tackled him from the side. The pistol went off and struck the back wall of the blacksmith shop as the two fell, with Hewey landing on top. Murphy lost his pistol when they hit the ground, and it fell almost underneath them.

Over the years Hewey had been in only a handful of fistfights and had been drunk for most of them. He had never really developed much skill or desire for fighting. Murphy, it quickly seemed, had practiced some. Lying flat on his back he dodged Hewey's first clumsy punch, then shot a quick jab that struck Hewey in the nose. Blood spurted from his nose, and his vision blurred.

Hewey was momentarily stunned by the blow, and Murphy grabbed him by the hair and jerked him sideways and to the ground. Murphy paused for a couple seconds to look for his pistol, then spotted it next to Hewey, only a couple feet away. Murphy dove for the pistol and had just touched the grips when he heard the unmistakable sound of a single-action Colt revolver being cocked, and within feet of his head.

"You turn loose of that pistol or I'll kill you right there," said Baker. When Hewey had gone for Murphy, Baker went for his own pistol, which was still on the ground where he had been forced to drop it.

Murphy, on his hands and knees, slowly retrieved his hand from his fallen pistol. He turned to look at Baker just as the old Ranger stepped forward and kicked him square in the face with the top of his right foot. There was an audible pop that Baker hoped was Murphy's jaw. The Pinkerton fell on his side and did not stir.

Baker blew the dust out of his pistol but kept it in his hand in case Murphy came to. "Hewey, you better pick up that pistol beside you, then bring me a length of pack rope."

Still addled from the shot to the nose, Hewey picked up Murphy's pistol. His nose was bleeding and he felt confused. He looked at Wilson, who lay on his back with Thomas opening his shirt to look at the wound.

"Hewey!" Baker barked. "Get some rope or we're gonna have to fight this son of a bitch again in a minute. I'll help with Wilson."

Hewey struggled to get to his feet, but his senses and strength were quickly returning. He remembered a pile of rope in Thomas's shop, so he set off for it at a quick walk. He wasn't certain he was steady enough to run yet.

Just past the corner of the building he met Daisy coming at a run, followed closely by Martha Thomas.

"We heard shots!" said Daisy, glowing. "Is everyone all right?"

Hewey didn't know what to say. She was about to see anyway. "No, ma'am. Bob got shot. I don't know how bad yet."

Daisy let out an agonized moan, then set off again.

Martha looked at Hewey and only said, "Harold?"

"He's fine, ma'am," Hewey said, then went into the shop. He found the pile of rope, and pulled out a piece that was several feet long. He trotted back, where he found Baker still standing near Murphy, who was beginning to stir.

Martha Thomas and Daisy were kneeling beside Wilson, working on him as best they could. Martha had ripped off the bottom of her own dress, and she was pressing the worn material onto the bleeding wound in Wilson's chest.

Hewey pulled his Barlow knife from his pants pocket and cut the rope in two. Baker kept watch while he tied Murphy's hands behind his back and then tied his feet together. It was not perfect, but it would do for the time being.

"I'm going for the doctor," Hewey said. "I seen the building in town."

"Hewey." Martha looked up. "The doctor lives in the little brown house behind his office, if he's not there. Tell him to please hurry."

"Yes, ma'am. I'll bring him."

He quickly stepped up onto Biscuit, then grabbed the reins to Baker's big bay. "It'll be faster than gettin' his." Baker nodded. Hewey nudged Biscuit into a trot, pulling on the bay's reins, urging it into a trot, then a lope when they were clear of the building.

Just as he hit the main street he met Sheriff Darnall coming at a fast lope. Both pulled to a stop in the center of the dirt road.

"What happened?" Darnall asked, halfway out of breath. "I heard a couple shots from around here somewhere."

"That banker shot Bob Wilson," Hewey said hurriedly. "I'm goin' for the doctor. Baker is behind the blacksmith shop. Got Murphy tied up."

"How about the banker? Does Baker have him, too?"

Hewey began moving off toward town but looked back.

"Mr. Thomas hit him with a pair of tongs. Pretty sure he's dead."

"What!?" asked the sheriff, but Hewey was gone.

CHAPTER EIGHTEEN

The doctor's office was located on the main thoroughfare through town, near one of the cafés Hewey preferred. That was the only reason he had seen it before. It was part of a simple wooden building that held three businesses. The doctor's office was in the center, flanked on one side by a small pharmacy and on the other by the undertaker's office.

That, Hewey thought darkly as he reined Biscuit to a stop in front, *is some good planning. One way or the other, nobody has to travel far.*

The sign in the front door said CLOSED, but Hewey tried the knob anyway. The sign was correct. The door was locked.

He hadn't even bothered to tie Biscuit. The reins were draped over his neck, and the bay's reins were wrapped once around the saddle horn. Hewey quickly stepped back in the saddle and trotted around behind the building, looking for the doctor's house.

The house was painted a light brown with black trim.

There was a low wooden fence around an immaculate yard, complete with some small trees and a flower bed along the front of the house. Hewey left the horses just outside the gate and jogged to the front door, which he began to bang on with his fist.

A minute later a man about Hewey's own age who looked as if he spent more time indoors than out opened the door and appraised him.

"A simple knock would have sufficed."

"A man's been shot down at the blacksmith shop. He's hurt pretty bad. I need you to come with me."

The doctor looked behind him, where a woman and two children were sitting at a table eating their supper. The doctor seemed to give it all some thought. "Very well. Let me go get my buggy and I will be right there."

"No, sir," Hewey said brusquely. "I brung you a horse. We don't have time for no buggies."

The doctor frowned, obviously not liking the situation. "Fine," he said, then shut the door in Hewey's face. Only a few seconds later it opened again, and the doctor was wearing a small hat and carrying a black leather bag that Hewey hoped carried some sort of doctor tools.

Hewey had to hold the doctor's bag as the man clumsily mounted the big bay horse. It always amazed Hewey that there were folks getting by and even prospering who had no horse sense whatsoever. The doctor seemed to be one of these.

"You ready?" Hewey asked when the doctor was situated.

He started to hand the bag back to the doctor but noticed the man was holding the reins with one hand and the saddle horn with the other. Hewey kept the bag.

"Yes. I am ready." The response was curt. He felt the vibe emanating from Hewey.

Leading the way, Hewey hit a trot. He would have preferred more speed, but a look back at the bouncing doctor forced him to hold it to a trot. He didn't think there were *two* doctors in town, in case this one hurt himself. He slowed slightly until Biscuit was alongside Baker's big bay.

He looked over at the doctor, who seemed determined if uncomfortable. "You makin' it all right?"

"I will be fine, sir. I ordinarily drive my buggy. I am saving my money for an automobile, which I hope to purchase before the end of the year."

Hewey only frowned. It was the first time he had ever thought an automobile might be preferable.

It took only a few minutes for Hewey and the doctor to reach the blacksmith shop, where they found Martha Thomas and Daisy still sitting over the unconscious Wilson. Daisy held a bloody cloth to the wound. Thomas still sat on the ground nearby, watching in silence and a sort of stupor.

Sheriff Tom Darnall had traded the rope tying Murphy's hands for handcuffs but had left the supposed Pinkerton detective's feet tied. Murphy was propped against a fence, his jaw swollen. Darnall stood nearby, keeping watch.

Booker lay as before, untouched.

Baker was outside Thomas's small saddle house, harnessing an old sorrel horse they had seen the Thomases use when they drove their buggy into town.

The doctor took it all in quickly, then jumped from the horse and rushed to Wilson. Hewey scooped up the bay's reins and went to help Baker. He didn't know what else to do.

The doctor tenderly placed a hand on Martha's shoulder. "Mrs. Thomas? Let me see, please."

The wound was just below Wilson's right nipple. The doctor gently rolled Wilson onto his side, peeking at his back. There was an ugly exit wound there.

"Inside my bag are some white towels," he said to no one in particular. "Hand me two of them."

Daisy quickly looked through the bag and found the small towels. She handed two to the doctor, who folded them into small squares and placed them over the wound.

"There is a roll of tape in there."

Daisy found it and began to hand it to the doctor.

"Tear me four pieces about six inches long."

Hewey and Baker had returned with the sorrel horse that they had hooked to a light wagon with one seat and a flatbed. Both watched the doctor working, and his efficiency was not lost on either.

Daisy handed the tape to the doctor one piece at a time, and he taped the towels to Wilson's back, covering the wound. He eased Wilson onto his back again, then repeated the process on the chest wound.

"I need to get him to my clinic." He looked directly at Hewey. "Help me get him in the wagon."

They loaded Wilson into the wagon as gently as they could, but the young man still moaned strangely at times. Hewey wondered if that was a good sign or not. He figured there might be hope if Wilson still had the strength to moan, but it sure did sound bad.

The doctor's name, Hewey learned later while they waited, was Frank Jenkins. His wife had sent for his nurse, who was waiting for them at the office when they arrived with Wilson. Hewey and Baker helped carry Wilson inside, then everyone was ushered out of the building.

After half an hour Hewey and Baker walked down to a little café because they knew it would be closing soon and they had not eaten since a light dinner out of their saddlebags.

Daisy Baker and Martha Thomas sat together on a wooden bench on the porch of the doctor's office, talking quietly to each other at times. Thomas sat alone on the edge of the porch, staring at the ground and speaking to no one.

Hewey and Baker had long since returned when Dr. Jenkins finally emerged. It was fully dark outside but some light came through the open door behind him.

Martha was the first to speak. "Tell us, Frank." She attended church with Jenkins and his family, so she knew him well.

Jenkins stood holding the towel he had been using to dry his hands. "He's alive."

Thomas, still on the edge of the porch in the darkness, let out an audible sob, the first sound he had made in two hours.

Jenkins shot a worried look toward Thomas, then went on. "The bullet broke four ribs, two in front and two in back. It creased one lung, but I believe it will be all right. There is considerable muscle and tissue damage. I sewed him up as best I could."

"So do you think he will recover?" asked Daisy.

"I believe that if he makes it through tonight, and we can keep him from getting an infection of some sort, he will make it. It's going to take some time, though.

"He's asleep right now and needs to stay that way," Jenkins went on. "One of you can stay, but the rest of you need to go on home. There's no sense sitting out here all night."

Daisy and Martha looked at each other, then Daisy said, "I'd like to stay, if it's all right with you."

"Yes, it is," Martha responded, taking Daisy's hand. "But you come for me if anything changes. Anything at all."

Martha walked down the steps and stopped in front of her husband. "Take me home, Harold," she said quietly.

Thomas stood, then walked up the steps and stopped in front of Jenkins. He stuck out one of his big work-hardened hands. Jenkins paused. Martha had always been friendly to him, but her husband had said little over the years. The doctor held out his hand. Thomas shook it firmly and nodded his head at the doctor, then turned and walked away.

Hewey and Baker saddled up and rode to the doctor's office at daylight the next morning to find both Harold and Martha Thomas already there. Unable to sleep anyway, the couple had walked the short distance earlier. Daisy heard them all talking outside and came out the door. She smiled at them.

"Bob was awake for a while earlier," she said. "He said he hurts terribly but doesn't feel too bad otherwise."

Martha hugged Daisy. "That's just great, dear," she said. "Why don't you let me take over for a little while? Let these boys buy you breakfast somewhere."

"I'll do that, but I'll be back soon," Daisy promised.

They found Sheriff Darnall in the café, along with several other older local men. They chose a table near enough to the sheriff where they could speak easily.

"How's your friend makin' it this mornin'?" Darnall asked.

Hewey answered for the group. "He's doing better, seems like. Daisy stayed with him all night and said he was talkin' earlier."

"I'm glad to hear it. I honestly wasn't sure how that was going to turn out."

Hewey and Baker both shook their heads. They had not, either. Baker looked over at Darnall. "Did you ever hear anything back from the Pinkertons about Murphy?"

"Not a thing. Sent that telegraph, but they never responded. First thing this morning I'm going to try the Pinkertons again and then talk to the marshal in Green Ridge. We'll get this sorted out somehow. The court will have to get involved, I guess. I don't know who will get to try Murphy—Laramie or Green Ridge. I'd choose us, since it seems to me it would be easier to prove and I'd like to send him to prison, or hang him."

Thomas had woken from his stupor of the evening before, but he had still been unusually quiet. "How about me, Tom? I guess I killed that feller yesterday."

"Legally speaking, you're in the clear. It was justified," said the sheriff. "Now, speakin' personally as your friend, I can tell you're bothered by it. That feller had just shot Bob right in front of you. They were probably about to shoot Hewey and Hanley here. Let it go, if you can."

"Thank you, Tom," said Thomas. He knew all those things already but was still relieved to hear it from Darnall.

The sheriff was done with his breakfast and stood. "I'll keep you in the loop on all this. I reckon we'll need some or maybe all of you to testify, but I can't say when or even what state that'll happen in."

He went to the counter and paid. He came back with a bowl covered with a small towel. "Breakfast for my prisoner. Oatmeal. It looks like his jaw is broken, but I'll get the doctor to look at him later this morning. He was complaining earlier, said you kicked him."

Baker didn't show any sympathy whatsoever. "Son of a bitch is lucky I didn't kill him. You can tell him that."

The morning air was cool two days later when Hewey woke before daylight. For some reason it gave him the itch to move on. It was a feeling he knew all too well. It had been visiting him every so often for going on twenty years.

Hewey and Baker found Wilson sitting in the morning sun on the porch of the doctor's office. He looked drawn and pale but far better than the last time they saw him. They drew up their horses and studied him.

"You supposed to be up and out here?" Hewey asked him.

"I don't know." Wilson grinned. "I didn't ask."

Baker stepped down and walked to the edge of the porch. "You sure had us worried for a while there," he said. "Why in the hell did you keep taunting Booker 'til he shot you?"

"I didn't really think he was going to shoot me, not then. I knew they planned to somewhere else and soon. I was just tryin' to mess with them, to force somethin' to happen so maybe we could get out of that jam. I guess it worked, sort of."

Wilson laughed at himself briefly then grabbed at his broken ribs. "Damn that hurts," he said.

"You're lucky to have got off that easy," said Baker.

"What are you gonna do now that you're a free man?" asked Hewey. "You ought to catch up that gray and come to Canada with me."

Wilson cut his eyes at Baker. "Well, I thought I might like to stick around here for a while and visit Daisy some more. We've talked about it."

Hewey groaned theatrically. "Oh hell, before we know it she'll have you farmin' or something else just as sad."

"No, Mr. Thomas was here yesterday. They want me to stay with them until I'm healed up, and then he wants me to work with him in the shop. Said he's gettin' too old and needs the help. I like it here. I think I'm going to do it."

"Don't hurt none that it's right down the road from Daisy, either, does it?" taunted Hewey.

Wilson smiled sheepishly, and Baker frowned at him.

Hewey was enjoying himself. "You sure you want to be a

horseshoer?" he asked. "You know what they say, about why there are no horseshoers in hell?"

Wilson shook his head. "No, why?"

"They get a pass 'cause they've already done their time," Hewey said.

Even Baker had to laugh, but then he grew serious again. "Bob, I think a lot of you. You're a good kid, turns out. Daisy is the closest thing to a daughter I'll ever have. You make her unhappy, even a little, and I'll put you back in that doctor's office in worse shape than you're in now."

Wilson couldn't tell if Baker was joking or not. "Yes, sir," was all he said.

◆◆◆

"It's time for me to travel," Hewey said to Baker as they rode back toward the blacksmith shop.

"I know. I been feelin' it comin' off of you. I appreciate you seein' this deal through with me, though."

Hewey dropped his reins so he could roll a cigarette. "There wasn't never any doubt about it. You know that."

"I do. But I appreciate it all the same."

"You're not comin' with me, are you?"

"No, I'm going to stick around, make sure this deal with Murphy and Wilson gets done right. I can't leave 'til it's over. I just can't help it."

Hewey looked at Baker, a knowing grin on his face. "You sure there ain't anything, or *anybody*, else keepin' you here?"

"What are you talkin' about now?"

"You don't reckon there's anything you need to check on over in Cheyenne, do you? You might need to do a little more *investigatin'* over there, maybe on that lady with the freckles?"

Baker couldn't help but grin himself. He was caught and knew it. "You know, you could be right. I might better ease over there and look around. Might even spend a little time while I'm there."

"Just be careful she don't get too tight ahold on you. You've stayed free this long. It'd be a shame to give it up now."

They found Harold and Martha Thomas sitting in the shade on their front porch watching them approach. The couple had been staying close together since the incident behind the shop, but Thomas had regained much of his fire.

"What's the news, boys?" Thomas asked. "I can tell you have something."

"Wilson was up and sittin' on the porch when we got there," Hewey said.

Daisy emerged from the house. She had come over to bathe, since the doctor's office was sparse on amenities. "He is not supposed to be up!"

"Easy now. He's all right," Hewey said. "And your uncle told him he'd kill him if he's mean to you."

"Uncle Hanley, you better not have!"

"Well, I didn't, exactly."

Hewey stepped off Biscuit and went to the porch. "Mr. Thomas, Mrs. Thomas, I'm headed out of here. I set off to see Canada, and I'm determined. I appreciate all you've done for me . . . for all of us."

Thomas pulled a roll of bills from his pocket and began counting it. Satisfied, he handed it to Hewey. "That will get us square, I believe. I'll loan you that sorrel if you want. You can drop him off here on your way back through, whenever that is."

"Oh, I better not. A polar bear might eat him and then I'd owe you for a horse. Ol' Biscuit can make it just fine. But thank you for the offer."

"You can take Little Jim to carry your grub," Baker offered.

"Now that wouldn't be a bad plan," Hewey said. "If a polar bear ate him it wouldn't be much of a loss."

"I have a question for all of you, before you go," said Martha Thomas. "Everyone seems to agree that those men robbed the bank and framed it on Bob. But as far as I've heard, no one has found the money. Is that correct?"

"I asked the sheriff about that yesterday," said Baker. "He believes Murphy and Booker hid it somewhere, but Murphy isn't tellin'. Probably never will."

Hewey shook hands with Daisy and then Thomas. He reached to shake with Martha, and to his discomfort she hugged him instead.

"You come back here anytime, Hewey," she said.

Hewey tightened his cinch one notch, then stepped up onto Biscuit. He had already packed his few possessions into his saddlebags and the war bag he tied over his bedroll. He was set to travel. He reached over and shook hands with Baker.

"I'll see you again somewhere," Hewey said.

"You stay out of trouble the rest of the way."

"Oh hell, why does everybody keep tellin' me that?" He turned Biscuit and trotted through town and on, headed nowhere but north. He felt a few small pangs of sadness at leaving his friends behind, but it was soon replaced by excitement when he rode into country he had never seen before.

CHAPTER
NINETEEN

Hewey had been following a wagon road in a northerly direction for about six days since leaving Laramie. It was beautiful country with grass-covered flats and what he had learned from a couple miners he met on the road were the Bighorn Mountains. It was the sort of country where Hewey thought he might like to spend a summer on a cow outfit, but he had the feeling the winters would not suit him.

He trotted into Sheridan early in the evening, low on supplies and conversation. Biscuit was an accomplished listener but a poor conversationalist, in Hewey's opinion.

Many of the buildings in town were connected to each other, sharing walls and a single roof. Hewey rode by the courthouse and a large, recently completed building that he learned from the sign outside was the new hospital.

Times are sure changing, he thought to himself before moving on.

He found a two-story saloon that stood alone, apart from the other buildings, as if the townspeople did not want it or its customers tainting the rest of their fair city. A saloon in town was permissible. Having it located next to the dry goods store or barbershop was not.

Hewey, undaunted by these finer points of etiquette, walked into the saloon and stood inside the door for a moment to get his bearings. The bar itself was built along the back wall, and there were a few small square tables scattered across the room between the front door and the bar. There was a staircase along one wall that led to a small landing and beyond that a closed door. To Hewey's practiced eye, it looked very much like a hundred other saloons he had visited previously. The patrons might change somewhat from place to place, but saloons were mostly just the same, one after the other, with the same end result.

Two of the small tables were occupied, one with what looked to Hewey like a couple local businessmen and the other by a pair of men who were likely laborers of some sort. Hewey knew only that they were not cowboys, so his interest moved on.

The bartender stood at one end of the bar, and toward the other end lounged a lone customer. Hewey was about average size, he had always figured, and he could tell at a distance that this stranger towered over him by several inches and outweighed him by well over fifty pounds. Hewey guessed him at about his own age, midthirties or so. The giant was dressed like a cowpuncher, albeit slightly different from those Hewey had been around. His hat was creased different, his spurs looked shiny and new, and he wore a pistol in a holster on his hip. Most of the cowpunchers Hewey was acquainted with carried their pistol in their saddlebags, if they owned a pistol at all. Hewey shrugged to himself, attributing it to his being far from home.

Hewey ordered a beer and slid two coins across to the bartender. He picked up the drink and regarded it for a moment.

"Howdy, stranger! Haven't seen you around before. You just passing through?" The voice was loud and demanding, though not necessarily unfriendly.

He looked down the bar toward the giant, who was smiling at him. Hewey had always tried to be friendly when he could, particularly to very big men in saloons.

"Sure am, mister, just passing through headin' north," Hewey replied as congenially as he could. He still wasn't certain if the big man was friendly or not. He noticed the two businessmen exchange a knowing look to each other, but he did not know what it meant.

The giant strode toward him, and Hewey thought for a moment of running for the door. He hesitated a second too long and the man was upon him. To his surprise and relief, the big man stuck out his hand. Hewey noticed it was the size of a plate with fingers as big as sausages. "I'm Wyatt Kelly. It's sure nice to meet you. I get the feeling we're going to have some fun."

Hewey shook his hand, slightly taken aback by the friendship that had been thrust upon him but still glad the giant wasn't throwing him through the door. "Nice to meet you. I'm Hewey Calloway."

"Finish your drink, and I'll buy you another. You don't mind, do you, Hewey? I know just what you need."

Hewey typically liked to ease into his drinking, which is why he had begun with a beer. It had always seemed to make the good times last longer. That did not seem to be the style of his new friend, so he gulped down half his beer.

"George," Kelly said to the bartender. "Set us up with a couple out of the good bottle, and leave the bottle."

The bartender filled two glasses, placed the bottle on the bar, and quickly retreated back to his place at the far end. Kelly didn't seem to notice. "Where you from, Calloway?"

Hewey told him he had spent the winter at a line camp in Colorado but was from West Texas. Before he could say more, Kelly cut him off.

"I was born in Ohio, but I come west on my own as soon as I could. I was born to work cows and ride broncs. You know how it is. Finish that whiskey and I'll pour you another."

Hewey did as he was told, still slightly afraid not to follow orders. He was feeling that old familiar feeling as the alcohol loosened him up, and he began to relax and enjoy himself. Even so, something in the back of his head kept telling him that not everything the big stranger said added up.

"Where all you worked, Calloway?"

"Well, mostly in West Texas, but I've spent some time in New Mexico and years ago we took a herd to Kansas."

"I have punched cows from Montana down to Mexico,"

Kelly cut in. His volume had been rising as the whiskey eased through his own system. Hewey wondered to himself if it took more whiskey for giants to get drunk.

"I never cowboyed in Texas. Most of those Texas boys are too big for their britches. Not you, of course. I can tell we have a lot in common, Calloway."

Hewey did not care for the britches remark and wasn't too sure about their commonality, but he was still sober enough to let it go in silence. Kelly gulped another shot of whiskey and slid another one to Hewey.

"Have another drink. The fun's just starting. Where you headed anyway, Calloway?"

"I'm just sort of takin' a trip, seein' some new country," Hewey replied. "I'm going all the way to Canada. I've never seen that country, and I intend to."

"I've been all over Canada. Nothing like it." The big man paused, for perhaps the first time since Hewey met him. "Tell you what, Calloway. I've been thinking about drifting north myself. Might be I ought to just go with you. We'll ride up to Canada and look around, maybe do some hunting. You like to hunt? Good bear hunting in Canada. I've killed seventeen bears and all but two were grizzlies. That's what we'll do. Tomorrow morning. You and me."

Hewey looked over at the two businessmen, who were both openly smiling at him since they were behind Kelly. One winked at him, and then they got up and left.

"Well now," Hewey stammered, not certain what to say. "I'm not too good a travelin' partner. I can't cook to suit anybody, not even myself."

"Don't worry about that." Kelly was smiling down at him. "I can cook anything you want. You tote the firewood and wash the dishes, and I'll handle the cooking."

That did not seem like a bad deal to Hewey, and he was nodding in agreement. He couldn't help it. He was feeling warm and loose and the giant Kelly was grinning and staring at him, forcing him to say yes.

"Have another drink, Calloway. I'm going to step outside and relieve myself, and we'll talk about this when I come back. You ever been to California? Maybe we ought to just keep riding, circle around and see California after we go to Canada. You think about it. I'll be right back."

Hewey watched as Kelly went out the door, the top of his head not missing the doorjamb by much. He looked around at the bartender, who was watching him.

"What's the deal, here, barkeep? Who is this feller?" Hewey kept his voice down so he wouldn't be heard through the door.

"Cowboy, if you give me half an hour to go around town and take up a collection, I bet I can get you twenty, maybe thirty dollars. All you'll have to do is take Kelly there with you when you leave. Heck of a deal. You want it?"

Hewey tried to think that over, but his head was getting foggy. He could not understand why the bartender would pay him to take the big man with him. He was confused.

"Why would you pay me to take him with me?" he finally asked the bartender.

"Because we can't take it anymore. He rode into town about six months ago. Doesn't matter if he's in here, the café, the hotel. Wherever he is, he's talking, and he's bragging. He's relentless. But he's so big no one is foolish enough to call him out on it, not anymore. A cowboy from an outfit west of here laughed at him one night for telling some windy, and Kelly beat him unconscious."

"Damn," was all Hewey said, frowning at the thought.

"Please, mister, just take him with you. I might can get you fifty dollars."

Just then Kelly walked back in the door. "Let's have another drink, Calloway." The big man filled Hewey's glass as well as his own. Kelly began talking again, jumping from subject to subject. He said there were plans to build an electric train in Sheridan. Hewey didn't know whether to believe it or not. He didn't understand much about either trains or electricity.

Hewey was used to holding his own in conversations, if not leading them entirely. With Kelly he hardly got a word in. Kelly, he soon learned, had once thrown ninety-six heel loops without missing while dragging calves to the branding fire. On the ninety-seventh the calf kicked one leg out and Kelly gave up his position to flank, disgusted with himself for bringing one to the fire by one leg. He had also once topped off thirty head of raw broncs by himself in one day.

Hewey began then to understand why the bartender wanted so badly for him to take Kelly with him, and he also began to think there was no way in hell he could stand to travel anywhere with Kelly. He didn't even know if he could last the night. He had known his share of windy storytellers. Hewey didn't mind that. He had even been known to get a touch loose with the facts himself when it made a story more entertaining. But this fellow was outright lying to him, and he knew it. He was feeling a strong urge to get away, but he needed to figure a way to do it without arousing the giant's anger.

He began searching for a way out, but his brain was too foggy. He was having trouble following the conversation and plotting his escape at the same time.

"Tell you what, my friend," Kelly said. "Upstairs they have a couple ladies of the night, if you know what I mean. Real beauties. Now, one of them has taken a shine to me, so you'll have to go with the other one. How's that sound?"

"I don't know, Kelly. I feel like I need to find somethin' to eat," Hewey said. He did need something to soak up the alcohol, but he also thought he might slip away and make a run for Biscuit, if he could just get outside.

"No, no, we don't need to stop and eat. We can eat later. I'm personal friends with the owner of the café. He'll cook us something late, if we want something. Even if he's closed. Don't you worry."

Kelly put his arm around Hewey and began guiding him toward the staircase. Never one to be pushed around, Hewey resisted slightly. Kelly just smiled and pushed a little harder. Hewey gave in and walked up the staircase.

Inside the upstairs door was a small parlor with a couple old chairs with worn cushions. There was a small table with an empty vase. Long ago someone had attempted to make it nice before giving up in realization that their customers came for something other than parlor ambiance.

Kelly knocked on one door, then the other. A plump brunette with far too much makeup and a dress that wouldn't suit the churchgoers opened the door that Kelly had commandeered. She smiled up at Kelly. "Oh, sweetheart, I was hoping you'd come visit me," she said with what seemed more like resignation than enthusiasm. Hewey figured she could not have helped hearing Kelly downstairs and had been expecting this visit.

The door in front of Hewey opened, and a pretty blonde stood smiling out at him. She was wearing a sheer white dress, and Hewey could see through it in some interesting places. He thought she was the prettiest thing he had ever seen. He stood staring, lost in the moment until a giant hand slapped him on the back.

"I knew you'd like her." Kelly laughed. "I'll meet you downstairs later and we'll have another drink."

The blonde reached out and took Hewey by the hand and led him inside the room. There was an old, small bed with white sheets, an older wooden chest with two sagging drawers, a rod suspended from the ceiling with three dresses hanging from it, and a small window on the back wall. There was nothing else.

"I'm Lillian. What's your name, cowboy?"

"Hewey Calloway, ma'am. Nice to meet you."

"Where are you from, Hewey?" She sat on the edge of the bed and beckoned him to join her.

In a stupor from being drunk and temporarily lovestruck, Hewey took a step toward the bed but was jolted back to reality by Kelly's voice booming through the wall. Hewey tried to block it out, but the walls were too thin and Kelly's voice too thick. He was talking about his exploits in the cavalry during the Indian Wars.

Hewey paused and thought about that for a moment. Unless he had misjudged Kelly's age by a couple decades, he decided after some rough arithmetic, then the Indians had about all given up the fight by the time Kelly was born.

He looked over at Lillian, sitting on the bed looking so inviting. Then he thought of Kelly demanding to become traveling partners and head out together in the morning.

The thought of riding to Canada alongside Kelly was just more than he could bear. Hewey even shuddered slightly, thinking about it. He had never met a person so disagreeable to be around.

He made up his mind then, and he leaned toward the girl. She was expecting something different, but Hewey whispered as quietly as he could. "Ma'am, I've got to get out of here, and he can't know." He gestured toward the wall and Kelly beyond.

Lillian smiled and almost laughed, before catching herself. Hewey loved her even more for it. "Believe me, cowboy. I know what you mean. Alice over there, she *really* understands. She said she's going to have to charge him double 'cause he won't ever shut up."

Hewey pulled out a dollar and laid it on the bed. He looked Lillian over again, slowly and carefully, hating to go but hating the alternative even more.

"I'll make a little noise from time to time, might help you," the girl said as he eased across the room toward the door. He took a long look back at her, willing himself to remember the image, then slowly opened the door.

Moving slowly, he took a careful step toward the stairs, then another. The floor creaked loudly during an unusual moment of silence from Kelly.

"Go away!" Kelly shouted from inside. "She's busy!" Hewey quickly retreated back into the room, fearful Kelly was about to burst out the other door. He wasn't certain if he was more worried about Kelly becoming violent or Kelly wanting to stay friends. Neither sounded good to him.

He tiptoed as best he could, half-drunk in boots and spurs, across to the window, where he paused a second, hoping it wasn't painted shut or that it would squeak.

Surprisingly, it slid open easily, and Hewey smiled. He crawled out the window, carefully lowering himself until he hung by his hands. It was too dark to see what was below. He could not tell how far it was to the ground or what might be under him. Then Kelly laughed in the next room. Hewey's resolve hardened, and he let go.

He hit on his feet, but it was a surprise since he never saw the ground coming. He fell backward but was miraculously unhurt. Hewey sat up, then placed his hands on the ground as he pushed to his feet. His hands came up wet, and he could tell his pants were damp also. He was confused briefly, remembering the dusty street as he came into town. It hadn't rained recently, he was fairly certain. Then he remembered Kelly stepping outside to relieve himself earlier, and he knew.

"Son of a bitch!" he hissed, glaring up at the room where Kelly was having a good time.

"You all right, cowboy?" came a quiet voice from above. Hewey could see Lillian peering down at him, backlit in the window.

"Yes, ma'am. Thank you." He still hated to leave her.

He thought he was in love, but he could also remember feeling the same about other girls in that line of work. The love always seemed to wear off as the whiskey did.

Hewey slipped around to the front of the saloon, where Biscuit was still tied. He felt a moment of guilt that he had left his horse saddled and tied all evening, but he had never intended to stay so long. He untied the one rein that had been looped around the hitching rail, stealing glances inside the bar. No one was visible. He tightened his cinch, grabbed the horn with both hands, and quietly stepped into the saddle.

Hewey held Biscuit to a walk, staying quiet as best he could. He lamented the fact that he never ate a café meal and that he was leaving without replenishing his own supplies. Some things are worse than hunger, he reminded himself.

He headed north toward the edge of town, then thought better of it. He reined Biscuit down a small side street, hit a trot, and left town headed west. He sure didn't want Kelly to follow and catch him.

He would have liked to stop and brush out his tracks or hide his trail like an outlaw on the run, but it was dark and the fact was that he just did not know much about that sort of thing. Instead he hit a long trot and kept Biscuit in it. Soon his neck ached from turning and looking back, which was pointless in the darkness, but he couldn't help it.

"I swan, Biscuit," he said quietly, afraid his voice would travel. "I never run from a man before, not exactly, but I just couldn't stand the thought of listening to him for another minute. You'd have been sick of him, too, if he went with us. We'll rest later, but for now we need to put some miles behind us."

Dawn found them several miles west of town. They had been climbing since leaving town, and it looked to Hewey like there were far bigger mountains farther west. When it was light enough to see well Hewey stopped and built a small fire, taking care to use dry wood to lessen the smoke. He felt ridiculous being so cautious, but then he heard Kelly's voice in his head and kicked out his fire. The coffee was hot enough, anyway.

Hewey had the high ground, and he could see his back trail for a couple miles more. After a couple hours with no movement other than two cow elk, he began to feel better. He cinched up Biscuit and eased west, feeling more relaxed but not enough to stop for a nap.

He had been following game and stock trails all his life. In addition to meandering with the terrain, what they all had in common was water at one end or the other. He and the brown horse both needed water, and there had been none at the other end of this trail, so it had to lie ahead.

Somewhere.

At midmorning he found it—a windmill in the distance, its tower standing tall and the fan turning at a leisurely pace in the light wind. As he drew nearer, Hewey saw that the mill was new, the unpainted timbers barely graying. Its long horizontal pipe emptied into a water trough maybe a dozen feet in diameter and perhaps two feet deep. An overflow pipe just at the surface ran downhill and fed into a dirt stock tank, itself so new that it held only about a fourth of the water it could accommodate.

Hewey wondered idly whether the tank was leaking into the subsurface soil or simply had not yet caught enough water to fill up. Given the lazy revolutions of the fan, he decided that the mill and its catchment had fallen prey to the same late-summer doldrums that often led to shortages of windmill water back home. Whatever its limitations, it was not Hewey's well to worry over. He was just grateful for the water, drinking from the pipe as Biscuit slurped loudly from the trough itself. Hewey loosened the cinch a few notches so the brown horse could drink his fill.

When he remounted, he spotted a sizeable herd of cattle drifting in from the north. North was as good a direction as west for a while, he decided, and he pointed Biscuit toward the incoming cattle, holding him to a steady walk to avoid spooking the leery range beasts. The herd parted as it flowed around him, giving him broad leeway.

Some of the cows struck a trot when they passed, in a hurry to get behind and beyond him.

He turned in the saddle to watch the cows close ranks in his wake, effectively eliminating his tracks.

"Well, Biscuit, ol' Kelly ain't likely to've stayed on our trail this far, and he would've had to wait for daylight to pick it up in the first place. Still, it never hurts to be careful."

Biscuit perked one ear back as Hewey burst out laughing when he realized the absurdity of what he had just done, covering his tracks like an outlaw to hide from a man who simply annoyed him. But then he didn't make it a quarter of a mile farther before he turned in the saddle and looked over his shoulder, checking his back trail.

CHAPTER TWENTY

Hewey realized one afternoon several days later that he had become homesick, an ailment that did not often strike him but one that did come up from time to time. He didn't have a home, exactly, and he did not own a thing in the world other than what he and Biscuit were carrying at the moment.

But he had been thinking more and more about his brother, Walter, and his nephews, Cotton and Tommy. It had been a couple years since Walter's wife had given him a blistering lecture and told him to leave. She had never cared for Hewey's ways and was always frightened Hewey would pull Walter away and draw him back to his old cowboy life.

Hewey had left at Eve's insistence, and he regretted that he didn't say more to Walter and the boys before going. He even admitted, although only to himself, that he should have sent some word or written a letter. He wondered what Cotton and Tommy had become. They would be teenagers and changing fast, he reckoned. Cotton might even be leaving soon, heading out to see the world on his own.

"Biscuit, once we've seen all there is to see in Canada, maybe we'll ease back down to Upton County and see what the old place looks like. How's that sound to you?"

Biscuit twitched one ear but gave no further response.

For two days, Hewey had been drifting northwest toward a range of mountains with no clear reason except idle curiosity, one of his most common motivations. He had changed course slightly because the still-distant mountains included a strange feature he could not explain or even guess at. Hewey had been in mountains off and on throughout much of his life, but he had never seen anything quite like what he was eyeing in the distance, so he headed toward it.

Hewey had little idea where he was. He was sure he had never been this far north before, but he was at a loss to figure just how far he had come. He was uncertain as well what day this was by the calendar, or really even which month. Late summer was his best guess. The days were getting shorter, of that he *was* certain, and the night's chill lasted well up into the morning. Grass was setting seed and curing, though it seemed too early for such things by his Texas way of reckoning.

As he pondered those questions, it began to dawn on him that he was not alone; off to the east and headed his way he could see another horse and rider. The horse was a grulla, and its grayish dun cast tended to blend into the surroundings. The rider, however, stood out like a rose in a pile of ashes. A man did not wear a coat that red if he didn't want to be seen.

As the horse and rider drew closer, Hewey could tell that the man's distinctive coat was part of a uniform. He wore a flat-brimmed hat with a four-pinch crease, similar to the hats Hewey and his fellow soldiers had worn when they served with Colonel Teddy. Riding breeches and tall boots, a brown gun belt, and shoulder strap completed the outfit. The rider left several yards between them as he reined up, and Hewey took that as his cue to bring Biscuit to a stop as well.

The stranger sat square-shouldered and ramrod-straight, and Hewey saw him unlatch the flap on his military-style holster.

"I don't mean you no harm, mister. The name's Hewey Calloway, and I'm not wanted for anything, if that's what you're thinkin'." The last comment wasn't exactly truthful, because there was that one as-yet-unforgiven episode of minor hell-raising on a certain New Mexico night a few years back, but Hewey reasoned he was nowhere near New Mexico.

"My name is Hardinger," the stranger replied, "Sergeant Caleb Hardinger of the North West Mounted Police."

"Well I'll be damned," Hewey blurted out happily, "a Mountie! Last I heard, you fellows were supposed to be in Canada."

"We are and I am," Hardinger said. "And so are you. I'd wager you've been in this country for several days now. You crossed the border over two hundred miles south of here."

Surprised, Hewey turned back and looked south. "Canada! Well, I never . . . The farthest north I've ever cowboyed before this trip was Wyoming, and that was a long way from home."

"Just where is home for you, Mr. Holloway?"

"Calloway," Hewey corrected him. "Hewey Calloway, and I'm Texas born and bred. Ain't never met a Mountie before."

"No, I wouldn't think so, and I've met only a few Texans, some to my regret."

Hewey noticed that as he talked, Hardinger had pulled a tally book out of a coat pocket. He paused to leaf through it. "Calloway, you said?"

"Yes, sir, Hewey Calloway."

The Mountie found the page he wanted, read it carefully, then put the tally book back in his pocket. His demeanor warmed slightly, and he eased his horse closer. It was the same change Hewey had often seen in Sheriff Wes Wheeler back home. He was still a lawman, and wary, but not quite so wary as before.

Hewey breathed a little easier. He hadn't realized until then that he'd been holding his breath. The reason, he reckoned, was probably concern that the little New Mexico misunderstanding might have made its way into the fugitive books of Canadian lawmen despite the time and distance. It was a silly notion, but Hewey had discovered long ago that those silly notions were sometimes his best.

Never at a loss for words, he decided Hardinger might tolerate a question.

"What the hell is that out yonder?" Hewey asked, pointing northwest at the feature he had been studying all day. "It looks sorta like a snowcap, but it's filled up a whole valley. I thought snow was supposed to be on the top of the mountain."

"That, Mr. Calloway, is a glacier, a solid mass of snow and ice."

Hewey was both surprised and excited. "Well, I'll be. I've heard about glaciers but never thought I'd see one. I guess you go far enough, you'll see just about anything. I had to come all the way to Canada, but I've seen a glacier now."

"You could have seen one in the States if you'd drifted a little farther west. They have them there."

"Oh, well," said Hewey, "I always like to see new country, and Canada is sure enough new country to me. Wish I could hitch onto one of those glaciers and drag it back home. We could use all that snow and ice in West Texas."

"You might give it a try," the Mountie said with a hint of a smile. "I've heard you Texas cowboys will rope just about anything."

"I've been known to dab a loop onto a few things I should've left alone." Hewey grinned. "Believe I'll just pass on this one."

Hardinger chuckled. "With experience comes wisdom, Mr. Calloway," he said with a touch of a finger to his hat brim. "Now, if you'll excuse me, I've miles to cover yet. You're not in my book, so I don't consider you a threat to the dominion of Canada. Good luck to you."

"And the same to you, Sergeant. Don't reckon we'll have occasion to cross paths again."

The Mountie struck off westward at a long, ground-eating trot. Hewey was impressed by the way the grulla horse traveled and watched until they disappeared over a rise.

Hewey hooked his right leg over the saddle horn, relaxing. He rolled a cigarette and lit it with a match from his shirt pocket, then watched the smoke drift with the northerly breeze. He sat quietly, staring across the browning grass at the glacier and mountains beyond.

Slowly, Hewey unhooked his leg and picked up the reins. He eased the horse around until its nose pointed southward.

"This sure is purty country, Biscuit, but I'll bet it don't look worth a damn under ten foot of snow."

He turned in the saddle to take one last look at the glacier, then straightened himself and touched spurs lightly to the brown horse.

"Let's go home."

A NOTE FROM JOHN BRADSHAW

Steve Kelton was my editor at *Livestock Weekly* for many years. He was my mentor and friend. Elmer Kelton has been my hero as far back as I can remember. Steve was working on *The Familiar Stranger* when he passed away in March of 2022. Steve's wife, Karen, gave me the honor of completing the manuscript.

Our only living child, Boone, died in an accident on January 9, 2023, five days before his sixth birthday and about two weeks after I finished *The Familiar Stranger*. Boone was a creative boy with many talents, not the least of which was his ability to tell a tale. He was a natural and gifted storyteller. Better than his dad.

The night after Boone died I had a dream, or perhaps more of a vision. I saw Steve walk up to Boone with Elmer a step behind. Steve looked down at my son and said, "Come on, Boone. I want you to meet someone. Let's go tell some stories."

ABOUT THE AUTHORS

STEVE KELTON (1951–2022) spent forty-two years as an editor for the San Angelo–based *Livestock Weekly*. A West Texas native, he was the son of the late Western novelist and livestock journalist Elmer Kelton. During his youth, Steve spent as much time as possible on the McElroy Ranch in West Texas's Crane and Upton counties. Managed by his grandfather, Buck Kelton, the McElroy was where Elmer and his brothers grew up. Steve was a journalist and the author of the nonfiction books, *Renderbrook: A Century Under The Spade Brand*, a history of the Renderbrook Spade ranch in West Texas; and *Grassroots Heritage*, a commissioned history of the Texas Farm Bureau's first fifty years.

JOHN BRADSHAW is a West Texas native and award-winning journalist who has written for the San Angelo–based *Livestock Weekly* for nearly twenty years. He is an avid horseman and a livestock producer. He lives outside the small town of Abernathy with his wife, Sara. This is his first book.

ELMER KELTON (1926–2009) was the seven-time Spur Award–winning author of more than forty novels, including the Texas Rangers series, the Hewey Calloway series, and the Buckalew Family series. He was also the recipient of the Owen Wister Lifetime Achievement award. In addition to his novels, Kelton worked as an agricultural journalist for forty-two years, and served in the infantry in World War II.